Cella

A Tale of Cinderella

Heartless

Copyright © 2009 Heartless
Cella, A Tale of Cinderella
Createspace
ISBN: 1478184264
First Edition

All Rights Reserved

This book is a work of fiction. Names, characters, places, and incidents either are products of the author's imagination or are used fictitiously. Any resemblance to actual persons, living or dead, events, or locales is entirely coincidental.

Dedicated to all my friends that have encouraged me to keep on writing.

IV

Table of Contents

Chapter 1	1
Chapter 2	4
Chapter 3	7
Chapter 4	21
Chapter 5	31
Chapter 6	38
Chapter 7	46
Chapter 8	52
Chapter 9	56
Chapter 10	61
Chapter 11	72
Chapter 12	79
Chapter 13	89
Chapter 14	94
Chapter 15	100
Chapter 16	106
Chapter 17	114
Chapter 18	117
Chapter 19	124
Chapter 20	129
Chapter 21	140
Chapter 22	146
Chapter 23	150
Chapter 24	165
Chapter 25	173
About the Author	181

Chapter 1

Once upon a time, as all good fairy tales start, there was a girl named Cinderella. She lived in the Kingdom of Bleu Evine with her father and mother. Her parents owned, in her opinion, the best bakery in the kingdom. They had a small flat above the shop that they lived in. She worked hard with her family, baking bread, kneading dough, creating sumptuous tarts, decorating cakes, and all of the other normal things that happen in a bakery. But they were still very poor, mostly because her parents were too generous with the homeless and poverty stricken. Because of their financial difficulty, Cinderella also had a job in the palace. She was only a scullery maid, and she worked even harder there than at the bakery.

The only person at the palace that did not like her was the queen. The petty reason for this dislike was because Cinderella had accidentally spilled a grape pudding on the floor and the queen had stepped into it before she had been able to mop it up. It had ruined the queen's favorite slippers and she was completely enraged. The queen was the absolute best at holding a grudge. She snubbed Cinderella whenever she saw her, and she also banned her from ever showing her face out of the kitchen. Regardless, Cinderella continued working there and did her best in everything.

Next door to Cinderella's parents' bakery was a dress shop. It was owned by a widow and her twin daughters. They were horribly snooty and very mean to everyone except those of noble birth and people that had large money purses. They especially hated Cinderella because she was always so well mannered, never bought their dresses, and was much prettier than the pudgy twins.

Cinderella wasn't really pretty; actually she was rather plain. But she had such a good heart that it shone through her ordinary looks and resulted in making her look far prettier than she really was.

She was of medium height, with plain light brown hair that was normally tied back in a braid. Her hazel eyes were round and not too large. Her nose was straight and neither too large nor too small. Contrasted to her neighbors, who were both short, fat, pug-nosed, and so ugly in their hearts it only served to worsen their appearance ten-fold, Cinderella was really pretty.

The neighbor girls were named Katherine and Angelica. Their hair was greasy black, their eyes were small and brown. Their lips were always twisted in a sneer, and their ears protruded oddly like strange leaves from the sides of their heads. They always wore the most fashionable, extravagant clothing made for them by their mother.

Their mother, Lady Hodgeshed, was a tall, bony woman. Her hair was prematurely grey and thin. Her nose was beaked like a bird of prey's and her fingers ended in long nails that curled like talons. She always wore grey or black, supposedly because she was in perpetual mourning for her late husband. However, she was the best dress maker that the kingdom had ever known and her clothing was worn far and wide by countless ladies of noble standing. Her heart was full of ambitious greed, not only for herself, but for her two daughters. She was always trying to pound lessons into their heads of how to be a proper lady, hoping that one day she could marry them off to some lord, duke, or even the prince. They liked to eat, lounge around the shop or their rooms while she made them dresses in her spare time. The would occasionally help their mother by tying a ribbon onto a new dress. In all, they were horribly lazy, and only their deceased father's wealth allowed them to get by in this manner.

Things continued on in the usual way of life. Cinderella was happy with her mother and father, endured the taunts of Katherine and Angelica about her shabby clothes, avoided the queen at all costs, and worked hard from sun-up to sun-down. Then one day a proclamation was made that would change her life forever.

Chapter 2

The sunlight was spilling over the ocean turning the sea-blue water gold.

"This is my favorite place in the world!" Prince Royal sighed, breathing deeply of the salty air as he leaned over the railing of his ship. Tomorrow, as long as the wind held steady, they would be in the port of Bleu Evine, his home.

"I don't entirely agree." said the young man beside the prince. He was the prince's personal valet and bodyguard. His name was Eric.

"Ah, but you are not burdened by the affairs of state like I am! You do not have to come out here to escape all that I leave behind me when I take to the seas!" the prince stated turning to his friend. The wind ruffled his long, black hair about his face and his deep brown eyes stared earnestly at Eric.

"Tis true. But I much prefer the solid ground beneath my feet over the pitching of the swells and the dangers the sea holds."

Royal laughed, "You are nothing but a landlubber, Eric!"

Eric smiled in reply and turned to watch the setting sun. He sucked in a lungful of the briny tasting air. "I suppose it does grow on one over time." he said softly. "At least the sunsets here are unparalleled to those on land

"I'll make you a seaman yet!" the prince exclaimed clapping him on the back.

Eric turned and, with an over-exaggerated bow said, "That is only if His Highness' parents will allow to be out here long enough to attempt such a thing."

The smile died from Royal's lips, "Yes, I suppose that is only too true. They will definitely not allow me to be out here very often." he turned from the railing and walked across the deck to his cabin. Eric stayed where he was.

Prince Royal loved the sea. His parents, though, hated it and were always upset when he left on one of his voyages. They had tried many things to keep him home on land, but he always found a way to leave. Royal knew that as soon as he showed up in port, he would be accosted with new things that his parents had come up for him during his absence.

Sure enough, when they made it into the bay the next morning and he had been driven to the palace in the elegant six-horse carriage, his mother met him with a large smile and a scroll of paper.

"Royal! How I have missed you, my son!" she hugged him and looked disdainfully at his long hair and coarse appearance. He had been gone for a year, his longest voyage yet, but she had still expected him to keep the proper appearance befitting a prince. She would have to have the royal barber pay him a visit.

"Hello, Mother." he hugged her back and smiled. "And what is that?" he asked motioning to the scroll, already dreading what it would contain.

"Oh, this? Well I was going to show it to you once you had rested and cleaned up. But if you want to see it now…" and she unrolled the scroll to show him what it said.

Royal Proclamation:

In honor of Prince Royal's return. His majesty, King Leander and Her Majesty, Queen Octavia, are holding a ball in his honor. Everyone is invited to attend, especially eligible, young ladies.

The ball is to be held the day following Prince Royal's return and will begin at sundown.

Their Majesties,
King Leander and
Queen Octavia

"Mother! I— you know how much I hate balls!" Royal cried out after reading it. He handed it to Eric who read it quickly and arched his eyebrow in wonderment. "And what was that part of 'eligible, young ladies'?!"

"My Son, it is high time to find a bride for yourself. At least your father and I are letting *you* pick." his mother ended pointedly.

Royal sighed, turned on his heel, and marched inside the palace. Eric hastened after him, letting the proclamation fall into the dirt.

Chapter 3

"Mother! Did you see the royal proclamation?" Cinderella burst into the back of the bakery.

"No, dear." her mother said as she put a batch of bread dough aside to let it rise.

"There is to be a ball, in honor of His Majesty, Prince Royal! Everyone is invited, Mother! And it said especially eligible, young ladies! Isn't it grand, mother! I would love to go to a royal ball! And to think that the prince has been away for over a year now, it is sure to be the most extravagant ball imaginable!"

"Yes, dear. Now why don't you help me with this cake batter." her mother was not unfeeling to Cinderella's excitement, she was just too preoccupied with the baking.

Cinderella calmed herself down and helped her mother until everything was completed and they could start on the supper preparations.

Once they had finished, they sat down to their meal of soup and bread. Her father had just closed the bakery, but he too had heard the proclamation.

"Wouldn't our dear Ella be splendid at a ball, Mother?" he asked as he sipped his thick coffee.

"Cinders would never be able to fit in with such a high level of society." was the curt reply.

"But, Mother! It is just a celebration. I am sure there will be plenty of people from our class as well!"

"I heard Katherine and Angelica are going to go." her father pointed out.

"Ha! Their mother would send them anywhere if she thought that it would expose those two to eligible bachelors."

"Mother, she is just wanting the best for her daughters." Cinderella said quietly as she dipped her bread in her soup. She didn't particularly like Mrs.. Hodgeshed but she could also understand where the woman was coming from.

Her mother looked over at her and replied, "As I want the best for you, my dear. I just don't want you filling your head up with wild ideas that will make you unhappy with this life. It is what we have and who we are. There is no getting higher than where we are. You're just a servant girl and daughter of two lowly bakers. No lord, duke, or prince is going to look twice at you. And I don't mean that unkindly, darling."

"Mother, I am not wanting to go to the ball to try to win someone! I want to go to experience a ball. To experience life in a different way than I ever will be able to have the chance to again! How many times do they allow commoners into the palace if they aren't servants?! And— well it would be a dream come true! I would still be content to go back to this life after that. At least I would have one lovely real dream to always remember for the rest of my life!"

"You truly want to go." her mother asked softly.

"Yes, my dear mother!"

"Then, if your father agrees, you may."

Cinderella held her breath and looked at her father. He smiled a large smile at her and said, "Of course you may go my dear, darling, Ella!"

"Oh, thank you, Mother and Father! Oh Thank you!"

"Your work at the palace won't interfere?" her mother asked sharply.

"Oh, no! The queen never wants me there late in the day. And she would definitely not want me at the ball as a maid, it would be too important an occasion! I would just go early in the day like I normally do."

"If that's the case, then, she won't be happy to see you as a guest."

"She won't know! And I will be mingling with so many other hundreds of people that no one will be able to spot me out from them all!"

"Well, you will need a new dress."

"I have thought of that. I can make up my old dress. I have a bit of money saved aside that I can go buy some ribbons and lace to sew on it. It won't be new, but it will still be pretty!"

"Well, let's talk no more of this tonight. We need to clean up and go to bed. Tomorrow will be a big day."

They cleaned all the dishes and went to bed. In the morning, as they sat down to their breakfast of porridge, Cinderella's mother announced, "Cinderella, your father and I decided that it will not do for you to go to a royal ball in your old dress. We have decided to… well, we want you to have a brand new ball gown!"

"Oh, Mother! Father!" Cinderella was so astonished she could hardly find the breath to thank them. "Oh, thank you, thank you!" she gushed as she hugged them both.

"You and I shall go over next door and speak to Mrs. Hodgeshed and see what she has available that is already pre-made." her mother stated as she hugged her daughter back.

"I can never thank you both enough!"

"Just have fun, and that will be enough." her father said. She hugged them both again and then she and her mother went to the Hodgeshed's dress shop.

"Good-day." her mother greeted the woman as they entered the shop. "Cinderella and I have come to look at some of your ball gowns. She is going to the ball tonight and—"

"Her! Go to the ball?!" Katherine butted in. Angelica sniggered.

"We need a dress." Cinderella's mother said addressing the twins' mother as if there had been no interruptions.

"Well, we have nothing that will fit Cinderella." Mrs. Hodgeshed replied in a haughty voice.

"But, this dress looks like it would fit perfectly!" Cinderella said as she fingered a silky blue gown that was hanging on display.

"That dress is sold. I haven't had time to take it down yet." The woman replied without even looking up to see which dress Cinderella was talking about.

"I'm sure that there is something here that would do for Cinder. Even if it requires a bit of refitting. I can handle that part, it's not like you would have to do any extra work to accommodate us."

"I just remembered! We have a nice coal dress in the kitchen that would work perfectly for her!" Angelica said while Katherine guffawed.

Cinderella couldn't hide the hurt that showed on her face. She walked over to her mother without saying anything.

"There are plenty of dresses here. I am sure not all of them are sold." her mother insisted, ignoring the cruel twin's words.

"I'm sorry ladies. There is nothing available for *her* here." Mrs. Hodgeshed said firmly.

""Very well then. So sorry to be a bother to you." Cinderella and her mother left the dress shop, crossing over to their bakery.

"Oh good. They're gone!" Angelica sighed and flopped down on a couch.

"Can you imagine that Cinderella wanting to go to the ball?! She would have just been an embarrassment to everyone there!"

"I'm glad you told them the blue dress was sold, Mother. She would have actually looked slightly pretty in it, and that would never do!"

"Of course not, girls. Katherine, Angelica, go get ready for tonight! There is a lot to do, and you will need all the time you can get to practice your dancing, arrange your hair, and get dressed in your gowns. You want to look your best when you are presented to the prince. We want him to get a good first impression of my lovely daughters. And don't squabble in front of him! Nothing is more unbecoming, and don't be jealous if he prefers one of you over the other. There is only one prince and he can't have you both!

The twins waddled off, arm in arm, laughing and talking.

☙

"I'm sorry, Cinder dear."

"That's all right, Mother. I suppose I will just fix up that old dress of mine after all."

Cinderella went to her room and pulled the old dress out of her trunk. It was coarse green with brown, ragged velvet trim.

"Oh, it's worse than I thought." Cinderella sighed. Her eyes wandered out of her window to the rooftop next door. She sighed unhappily, but she refused to be jealous of Angelica and Katherine. She dug through her trunk till her hand closed over the tiny silk pouch that held the few coins that she had been saving up to get something special. Now was the time to use it.

"Mother, I'm off to find some lace and ribbons." she called out as she walked past the kitchen door.

"All right, dear!" her mother called back as she pounded dough on the counter.

Cinderella walked out of the back door and wandered down the town streets. She knew where to go. A small market stall always had assortments of things to fix up dresses, most of it was rather cheap and she was hoping to have a little bit of money left over to still save for late.

As she was walking, the sound of terrified squeaking reached her ears. She turned and saw a group of boys in an alley. They were gathered around a tin washtub, and the squeaking was coming from inside of it. Cinderella's curiosity got the best of her and she walked over to see what was making the pitiful sound. The boys didn't notice her when she first walked up, they were too intent on what was going on to heed a newcomer.

What Cinderella saw filled her caring heart with pity. In the washtub were five, tiny grey mice. They were bunched up together squeaking in their terrified voices while a large, orange cat sat in-front of them. A dead mouse lay between its paws. As she watched, it reached out and batted one of the mice across the head sending it tumbling away from the others. The washtub was too slick for the mice to scramble out, and the cat was thrilled in being able to tease the little creatures.

"You boys should be ashamed!" Cinderella cried out.

The boys all turned at the sound of her voice."Ah, go away!" they said.

"No! You are all cruel boys to do such things to those poor mice!"

"We don't care! Fang hasta eat and have fun!"

"Well *Fang* can go somewhere else." And Cinderella scooped the massive cat out of the tub and dropped him on the ground. He hissed and tried to claw her, but she had dealt with plenty of bad cats all her life. There were always stray cats hanging around the bakery that her mother made her get rid. With the cat gone, she scooped up all five mice and deposited them in her pocket.

"Hey! You hafta pay for them!" the boys cried. "We paid to get them."

"I'm only taking them to release them somewhere safe." Cinderella said.

"No ya, ain't! You can't! Pay up, or you'll be in trouble for stealin' what we already paids for!"

Cinderella hated to, but she reached into her purse and produced a coin. "Here." she said and handed it to the presumed ringleader.

"We paid more'n this!"

"How much, truthfully, did you pay?" she asked, her hands on her hips.

"We all paid a coin a mouse."

"Well, since one is already dead then I only need to give you a total of five." Cinderella grimaced as she reached into her purse and produced four more coins. She handed them over to the boys and walked away. Now she only had three coins left, and she doubted that would buy very much ribbon or lace.

When she reached the market stall that sold the trimmings, she looked over the wares searching for something pretty, yet still cheap enough for her.

"Excuse me." She asked the owner, "Don't you have any lace for a coin? Or satin ribbons perhaps?"

"I'm sorry, Miss. But I'm all sold out. The cheapest that I have left all start at four coins."

"Oh," her face fell as she muttered a thank you. Cinderella left the stall and glanced quickly at a few of the other merchants' wares, but no one else carried what she needed. She left the market square very low spirited.

If only those nasty boys hadn't been torturing the mice! She knew she could never have left them to be murdered by that cat, and she was glad that she had been able to save them, but she was still disappointed that she wouldn't be able to fix up her dress now.

She walked out of town to the surrounding hillsides. She had decided that she would release the mice at the edge of the wood. She would never be allowed to keep them in the bakery.

She walked across the green hills and marveled at the beauty of the countryside. She rarely was able to go outside of the city since she was always busy working, but she loved the open expanses and the clean air and the freedom that she felt while being out there. She walked to the woods and knelt down to let the little mice go. They were all curled up, asleep in her pocket and she smiled at them. Very gently, she reached in and lifted the five tiny creatures out. As soon as she set them down they awoke. They started squeaking at her and scurried back into the folds of her gown. She laughed and set them in the grass again.

"Go on. You can find a new home now." she said softly. The mice turned back to her again.

"They don't appear to want to leave you." a cracked sounding voice said behind her.

Cinderella turned sharply and saw an old woman leaning on a walking cane watching her.

"Don't worry, dear, I am just an old woman that can't hurt anything."

Cinderella smiled, "I'm not frightened. I just wasn't sure who you may have been. I didn't hear you come up."

"I can still move silently. I know these hills very well. What are you trying to do with those mice though?"

"I can't keep them. You see I live in a bakery and my parents would never allow me to have anything for a pet."

"How did you come by them then? Or did you save them from your mother's broom?" and the old woman chuckled.

Cinderella smiled at the thought of her mother wielding a broom against the five mice, more than likely she would have been standing on a chair screaming for Cinders' father to come and get rid of them.

"No, no. They weren't there. I saved them from some cruel boys." and then the whole story came out, of her going to town to get trimmings for her dress because the neighbors would not let her buy one of theirs; how she met the boys, bought the mice, and then did not have enough money to buy any lace or ribbons. "And then I cam here to release the mice." she ended.

"Well, you do have a kind heart. What is your name, child?"

"Cinderella."

"Well, Cinderella, am I correct in assuming you won't be going to the ball now?"

"Sadly, yes. I could never go in my old dress. And I have nothing to fix it up with!"

"You, poor girl. Now I can help you out, just come with me." and the old lady hobbled away.

Cinderella dropped the mice in her pocket again and followed the woman. The old lady led her to a small, stone cottage. Ivy grew up the sides and a golden glow from the half opened window gave it a very enchanted, homey feel. Everything was very tidy and charming.

"Now child, I am the old servant to a Duchess who is nearly as old as I am. She has always let me do as I wish and borrow what I need or want from her. I can allow you to borrow a dress from her wardrobe, she has never worn it, and she never will since the style has gone out of fashion. I know it will still be quite becoming on you. Fashion is far over-rated." The lady had led Cinderella inside the cottage which was much bigger inside than it had appeared outside. They went into a room where three large wardrobes lined against the walls. The lady opened the first one and took a dazzling, deep purple dress out. It was lined in diamonds and the whitest of lace. Cinderella's eyes grew wide at the sight.

"I cannot borrow this! That is such a fabulous dress! I could never dare touch it!" she gasped. "Why it must cost more money than I could ever hope to earn in my lifetime!"

"Nonsense. You will wear it tonight. Now go on and take it and be the belle of the ball! I'll send a coach to pick you up at sunset. Don't say a thing to anyone at the ball as to where you got this dress, and do not worry your head over it! The only thing I request is that you leave the ball at midnight so I can make sure that everything is back in its place incase her ladyship decides to visit. She always comes before sunrise if I see her at all. I could never get in trouble with her and neither would you. But she does like to gab and I wouldn't want her spreading stories about you to the other noble families. I would just hate for her to embarrass you. Tonight you will be a princess!"

"You are very kind." Cinderella said, hardly able to believe this old lady would do such a thing for her. The woman wrapped the dress up in a drab cloth and handed the parcel to Cinderella.

"Now, about those mice." the old lady said.

"Oh, I nearly forgot about them!"

"I can take them for you. They will live in perfect luxury here. I love all animals and have a certain way with them."

"Oh, would you?!" Cinderella handed the five mice to the lady who laid them on a velvet cushion and found them a wedge of cheese. They happily started to nibble on it and then they fell into contented sleep.

"Thank you ever so much again!" Cinderella said joyfully.

"That's enough. You're welcome, and just remember midnight. Give the dress to the footman and they will bring it back to me."

"Yes, yes, I promise!"

Cinderella hurried home and left her parcel in her room. She didn't stop to speak to her parents and they hadn't seemed to notice her coming home. She left the bakery and quickly raced to the palace so she would not be late to do her cleaning for the day. When she entered the kitchen she was greeted by the head cook.

"Cinderella, didn't you get the message?"

"No, I haven't been home most of the morning. What is it?"

"Well… I'm sorry, the queen said that she did not want you to work at all today." the cook looked sorry to deliver the message and Cinderella understood immediately.

"I see. I suppose I shall leave then… Goodbye." she left the kitchen hurriedly before anyone could see the anger on her face. Queen Octavia just didn't want her to be working on such an important day thinking she would mess something up! And it was all just because of that sour grape pudding! Cinderella reached home and helped her parents in the bakery, of course they had already received the message for Cinderella not to come in to work.

"Dear, if you want to go fix up your dress go ahead. We can take care of everything." her mother offered.

"That actually won't be necessary mother. I met a lady who insisted I borrow a gown from her. Just wait till you see it!"

Close to sundown, Cinderella went to get changed. She donned the gorgeous purple dress and it fit her perfectly! She had pulled her hair into a bun, and what a surprise she found with the dress! Wrapped in the parcel was a diamond tiara. Cinderella placed it on her head, and was surprised at how different she looked when she had finished. She showed her parents and they exclaimed in wonderment at the lavish gown and the diamonds and tiara. They insisted on knowing who would allow her to borrow such a gown and she told them the story of the mice and meeting the old woman. Neither of her parents had ever heard of a Duchess' servant living out on the hillsides in the cottage. If not for the proof of the dress they would have thought that Cinderella had fallen asleep and dreamed it all.

Cinderella had already seen Katherine and Angelica leave with their mother to go to the ball and neither of them had a dress half as nice as hers. Whether it was out of style or not, she would be as dazzling as a princess! Her parents and she agreed that there was no way anyone would be able to recognize her.

The sound of a coach stopping outside the bakery sent them all to the door. Waiting to drive Cinderella to the ball was a fancy black carriage being pulled by a team of the most outstanding black horses. A footman hopped down and opened the door for her. She gathered up her layers of skirts and climbed inside. The footman bowed, shut the door, and climbed back up on his seat at the rear of the carriage. Then the driver lightly flicked the reins and the horses trotted smartly off. Cinderella waved to her parents and settled back on the velvet cushioned seat. Never had she dreamed of anything as fine as this!

Chapter 4

"Eric, give me a hand will you?" Royal called as he tried to straighten his robes.

Eric walked over and pinned the golden chain to the shoulder of Royal's tunic and straightened the robe out correctly. "You look fabulous, Your Highness."

Royal stared at his reflection for a moment and finally agreed. "I do so hate these gatherings! I abhor having to dance with all of those overly flirty women who have only one thing on their minds!"

"It really isn't so bad, Prince Royal." Eric said as he smoothed his own wavy brown hair down. "Anyway, for me it isn't." he added with a smile.

"Well, Eric, you like dancing. You also like the ladies. I do not care for either half as much as you. Besides, you do know what my parents are doing to me."

"Hmm?" Eric muttered absently as he kept messing with a lock of hair that would not stay in place.

Royal was still talking, not even paying attention to whether or not Eric was listening, "They are making me find a bride. If I don't, then they will pick one. And after I marry, I will have to stay here! I've never met a woman that likes the sea! They think this will finally make me settle down and they have finally found a way that they can force me to remain here with them."

"But you would be the one to have the say in whatever you wish and choose to do. So what if the woman you marry does not wish to sail, you still could by yourself, or command her to go with you."

"No, I wouldn't. Even though Father likes to think that he does have absolute control, Mother is the one that has the final say in almost everything. The only time she doesn't is if it is something directly involving the kingdom. Any personal, family matters, Mother decides it all."

"Well then you better find the girl! I'll keep my eyes open for the perfect match for you! Maybe we'll be lucky and find someone that actually enjoys ships and the ocean."

""Very well, Eric. You do that. She needs to be smart for I despise ignorant women, not too independent, and of course pretty. Ultimately I just need to be able to still go to sea when I wish too."

"Ha! You'll need to find a pirate princess then!"

"Fine then, I shall marry a pirate princess."

"You're parents would never allow it. Besides piracy is illegal so I'm sure she would be put to death or at least imprisoned."

"I know." Royal sighed. "Well, Mother is not going to be very happy if we tarry here any longer. You look quite fine, Eric. Quit mussing with your hair" and with that, Prince Royal turned and left the room with his ever faithful valet following.

The guests had already started arriving when Royal joined his parents in the ball room. The guests, specifically young ladies, immediately swarmed all around him chattering and laughing and batting their eyes. Royal groaned silently to himself, but kept a smile fixed to his face. His mother joined him and, wrapping her arm about his shoulders, whispered into his ear, "Princess Isadora from Lefye is quite a remarkable lady."

Royal glanced over at the princess and saw just another woman like any of the others. He had to admit that she was prettier than most, but that could also be attributed to her expensive clothes and the make-up that could disguise flaws so well. Her eyes were watery blue; her pale hair, which was almost white, was pulled very tightly away from her face enhancing her high cheekbones and sharpening her features far more than what they truly were. She coyly batted her eyes at him and smiled. He smiled a half sneer and turned away from her. The only people that were there at the moment were those of royal or noble blood. Soon the more "common" people started arriving. Royal sighed, he was tired already and wished that the evening was over.

Eric came over to him, "How's it going?" he mumbled.

"Tiring. Have you found anyone worthy enough? I still have not seen a single one!" Royal replied.

"Sorry, these princesses and Ladies are too far above me to even look at me, so how am I supposed to find one if I can't even talk to them?"

"That's fine, Eric." the prince smiled, "Well, everyone will be here soon and then I'm sure Mother will start the dances. Oh how I am not looking forward to it!"

Indeed the dances did start very soon. Royal found Princess Isadora nearby and he bowed and asked her dance, just to please his mother. Besides he would probably have to dance with ever single lady there before the night was over.

Isadora had the most horribly grating voice to his ears. She spoke so painfully smooth and quiet that Royal had to ask her to repeat herself every time she said something. She batted her eyes constantly and hemmed and hawed if he asked her any questions, never actually answering anything he said. The dance couldn't be over soon enough for him.

Royal glanced around for Eric and spotted him dancing with a plain commoner. She was smiling so bashfully that Prince Royal was afraid that she would start to cry or break down in a nervous fit for she looked nearly frightened to death. At that moment he heard a voice behind him and turned to see a tall, bony lady with grey hair and a beaked nose. Beside her stood two identical overweight girls decked out in gaudy dresses and jewelry. He bowed formally and the lady sank into a deep curtsey. She hit both girls discreetly and they too curtsied, though they wobbled dreadfully.

"Your Highness, I am so honored to meet you." the lady said. "I am Mrs. Hodgeshed and these lovely girls are my darling daughters, Katherine and Angelica."

The girls blushed and batted their eyes. Royal smiled in reply though he was retching inwardly.

"I was so hoping they could meet you! They haven't been able to rest a minute, so great was their excitement at the prospect of meeting the prince."

"Yes, and dancing with him and trying to marry him." Royal thought, but he only said, "It is always a pleasure to meet my subjects." he turned to the closer of the twins, not sure if it was Katherine or Angelica, and sweeping into a bow asked, "Would you care to dance?"

The girl giggled as she curtsied and took his arm. They went to the dance floor. They passed by Eric who was dancing with a pretty girl that wasn't concentrating on the dance at all, instead she was straining her neck to see the prince at all times. Royal couldn't miss the expression on Eric's face when he saw the girl that Royal was dancing with. He shook his head in over exaggeration of no. Royal smiled and nodded in agreement.

෴

Cinderella arrived at the ball and the footman opened the carriage door and held out a hand to help her out. She stepped gracefully down and stared up at the doors wide open for her to enter into the palace. She had been here countless times, but never before as a guest and never before for a ball. She swallowed nervously, thanked the coachmen, and ascended the stairs to the inside of the grand hall.

The guards at the door bowed stiffly. She smiled at them, wondering if they recognized her, and went into the corridor. She could hear the orchestra playing a beautiful dance number as she entered the ballroom. She paused and gazed in wonder at the gathering of people clustered about in their many colored dresses and fancy clothes. She felt out of place and hesitantly walked near a group of people. Everyone stared when they spotted her and whispers started to run around as to who this young lady could possibly be. Cinderella didn't recognize anyone except Mrs. Hodgeshed and her daughter, Katherine, she didn't see Angelica dancing with the prince.

She finally spotted him and she was immediately enraptured by his handsome face. She hoped beyond anything that she could dance with him. It would be the perfect night if she did. The dance ended and Cinderella stood around waiting, hoping the prince would see her and come over. He didn't even look her way. Some men came over and asked her to dance, but she declined them all. They walked off with sad faces until they found another pretty girl that would dance with them.

"Would the most beautiful lady here tonight care to dance with me? I know it is preposterous of me to ask since you are so apparently above my rank, but I just had to ask."

Cinderella turned and saw a rather nice looking young man beside her. His brown, wavy hair was flopping across his forehead, refusing to stay in place. His green eyes had a friendly look in them. He was dressed in finely tailored clothes, but Cinderella could tell he was not a nobleman. She glanced at the dance floor and saw the prince, now with Katherine, already starting the dance. She sighed inaudibly and turned back to the man.

"Yes, you may. But I must know who you are first."

He smiled, took her hand, and led her to the floor as he said, "I am Eric, the prince's Valet, bodyguard, and personal friend and confident."

Cinderella smiled and replied, "I am Cinderella and it is a pleasure to meet you, Eric."

He too smiled and said, "Cinderella is quite an unusual name. Please, tell me where are you from?"

Cinderella didn't know how to answer him, apparently he thought her a lady or even possibly a princess. She didn't want to lie, but she knew he would never believe her if she said she was from Bleu Evine, and she didn't really want to tell him that she was just a commoner. For one night in her life she could be more, and she wanted that desperately. Instead what she replied with was, "You would never believe me. So let it remain at that."

Eric decided to respect her wishes, but they continued to talk, and he liked her very well. Here was actually a girl that might be fit for Prince Royal! She seemed intelligent enough, he couldn't tell if she was too independent or if she had any love of the sea, but she was beautiful and warranted the prince's consideration. He intentionally danced closer to the prince and when they were alongside, he nodded his head emphatically at Cinderella. Cinderella didn't notice she was too busy staring at the prince and Katherine, who had apparently not recognized her. But Royal saw and he looked at Cinderella curiously. He had seen and met all royalty, so he thought, before the commoners had arrived and he knew he could not have missed someone like her. She noticed his gaze and blushed. The dance didn't end soon enough for either of them, and as soon as Prince Royal had taken Katherine back to her mother and sister, he found Eric, who was looking for him to introduce Cinderella.

"It is a pleasure to meet you!" Royal swept into a bow.

She curtsied beautifully and murmured, "It is a pleasure to meet you, Your Highness."

"May I?" he asked offering his arm.

She gracefully took it and they walked onto the dance floor.

Queen Octavia was watching with eagle eyes, she saw the very beautiful, presumed princess, and she saw the way her son appeared somewhat enraptured with her, as soon as they stepped onto the dance floor, she had a quiet melody begin, and the lights dimmed.

Royal and Cinderella danced beautifully together. Everyone talked in hushed tones about the couple, how good they looked together, and wondering, still, who she could be.

"Ella," the prince said, "It is all right if I call you that?"

"Of course." she replied softly, afraid she wouldn't even be able to respond.

"Who are you?"

"Cinderella."

"No, no, I mean who are your parents? Where do you come from?"

"You wouldn't believe me if I told you."

"Of course I would!"

"Please, I would rather not say."

Royal didn't press her, in her own time he would be able to get her to tell him.

He danced only with her the rest of the night and he introduced her to his parents as Ella. His mother was most gracious and did not recognize the scullery maid that she so hated. His father was most kind as well. But the night was getting later, and suddenly Cinderella heard the clock striking midnight.

"Oh, no!" she cried. "I must go. Excuse me!" she turned and ran from the room, everyone watched her in puzzled wonder.

Royal ran after her, calling for her to wait. Eric followed to give assistance if he could, but Cinderella had already gone outside and climbed into her coach. The driver whipped the horses into a gallop and Royal stopped, being left in the dust of the carriage. He sighed and Eric pulled up beside him.

"Well?"

"She didn't tell me where she lived or anything. She is most peculiar, and yet…"

"And yet you liked her?" Eric grinned.

"I believe very much so."

Eric led Royal back inside and he told his parents that he had been unable to catch her.

Later, after all the guests had finally left, the king and queen decided to have a talk with Royal.

"Son, we have decided to host another ball the night after tomorrow. She is bound to come back." his mother said.

"Wait, Octavia. Royal, do you even want to see her again?"

"More than anything, Father! I am almost positive she is the one! There was definitely no one else here this evening that caught my interest so much."

"Very well. Octavia you may take care of the ball, Royal do not be too disappointed if she does not come back."

"I know she will come back!"

"We will post the announcement tomorrow then." the queen confirmed.

Royal bowed and left. He informed Eric of his parent's decision who thought that it was a good attempt at bringing the girl back.

☙

Cinderella reached home and she hastily changed out of the gown and tied it up in its parcel with the tiara. She handed it over to the footman and watched as they drove away into the dark. Thankfully the Hodgeshed's had not arrived home yet so they had not seen her return. Cinderella related the entire evening to her parents, then she went to bed happily dreaming of dancing with the prince.

Her dream had come true and she couldn't be happier.

Chapter 6

The next morning the proclamation of another ball was posted. Cinderella heard and she hoped that she could go once again, but she didn't know how she could. Her parents would surely give her permission again. After all the first ball had gone so well, they shouldn't object.

She put the ball out of her head and decided to go visit the old woman. She wanted to thank her again for letting her borrow the dress and also see how the mice were. After she had completed her work at the palace kitchen, she hurried across the hillsides to the cottage.

"Hello, Cinderella!" the woman called out. She was sitting in a rocking chair that was set on a cobbled patio beside the cottage. She had a basket of thread with her was busy knitting.

"Hello!" she waved and hurried up to her. "I wished to thank you again! I had the most amazing evening! How are the mice? The prince danced with me nearly all night! Oh thank you, thank you!"

"You are most welcome, dear child. The mice are fine, I have built them a lovely little house of their own. Did I hear correctly that there is to be another ball tomorrow evening?"

"That is correct."

"Would you like to go again?"

"I would love to! But— well, I hate to ask…" she blushed, embarrassed that she was actually thinking about begging to borrow the dress again.

"It is not a problem, dear girl! Here, I already picked out the perfect dress for you." and the old woman set her knitting down as she stood up and let Cinderella inside the cottage. There was a drab parcel lying on a table in the front entrance. "I'll send the carriage at sunset to pick you up. Just remember midnight again, my dear."

"Oh, yes I will! I can never thank you enough!"

"Just go dazzle the pompous royalty and nobles!"

Cinderella smiled and took the parcel. When she got home, she found a deep blue gown trimmed in silver thread and sapphires. Matching, elbow length gloves and a silver and sapphire frontlet was also included. She touched everything gently. It was even more gorgeous than the previous dress!

⋆

The day of the ball had arrived. The Hodgesheds had left early once again. Cinderella readied herself and waited for the carriage. The same coachman and footman came, but the carriage was much different. It was open-roofed and silver with deep blue trim and seats. A team of four, elegant white horses were champing impatiently at the bit, and deep blue plumes adorned their headdresses.

The footman helped Cinderella in and she reclined back. She gazed out at the gorgeous sunset enjoying the feel of the wind as the carriage paraded her through the streets.

Royal was impatiently scanning the guests. He had Eric on the watch-out near the entrance for any sign of Ella. Finally, she arrived. Royal was even more astounded by her beauty this evening than the at the previous ball. He hastened to her and immediately asked her to dance with him. Everyone there was jealous. As soon as she arrived he ignored all of the other guests and no one else was able to get a dance with him.

She would still tell him nothing of where she came from. And once again, at the stroke of midnight, she ran from the palace to her waiting carriage. Royal failed to catch up with her, and was once again unable to know how to find her.

The next morning, a royal proclamation was posted throughout all of Bleu Evine and the neighboring kingdoms, requesting any information about the mysterious Princess Ella.

"My dear, you must go and explain to the prince about yourself." her mother said. This is what she had not wanted to happen to her daughter. Once the prince knew she was a commoner he might get very angry and think she had purposefully attempted to trick him.

"Oh, Mother, I can't! I can't! If I show my face to the prince— oh, please! Let us let it be. He is sure to forget all about me over time!" Cinderella was terrified. She shared her mother's fears that he might be angry at her. And she did not want to ruin the memories of those two nights by whatever may happen.

"Cinderella, you must." her father commanded. Cinderella knew she would have to now that her father had spoken. Everyone always did what he said. So she found her cleanest and least patched dress and walked to the palace. She entered the front gates and nearly ran into Eric who was standing right inside the gates, covered by the shadows.

"Excuse me." he said. He looked her over and asked, not unkindly, "Shouldn't you be using the servant's entrance?"

"I have information in regards to the girl, Ella. I must talk to the prince. Will you please let me speak to him, Eric?"

Eric started in surprise, "How-how did you know me?" he asked unsurely. Commoners would never know his name, and the servants did not know very much about him since he was almost always with the prince and did not speak to any of them very often.

Her cheeks bloomed bright pink as she realized her mistake, "I-I will explain all. Just please take me to talk to Prince Royal first."

Eric hesitated a moment, then agreed and led Cinderella to the room where Royal was waiting for any news to arrive.

"Your Highness, I have a girl here who claims to have information in regards to Ella."

Royal instantly perked up and looked expectantly at Cinderella. "Yes, what is it that you know?"

Cinderella swallowed nervously and took a step forward. She cast her eyes to the floor and whispered hoarsely, "I am Ella. Cinderella."

"What?!" Royal sprang to his feet from where he had been sitting. Eric was too shocked to even exclaim.

"It is true. I merely borrowed the dresses from a kind old lady because I had nothing fit for a ball. I was afraid to tell you that I am only a commoner because I thought that-that—"

"That I would not like you?" Royal interrupted.

Cinderella raised her face and looked him in the eyes, "Yes." she stated.

Royal gazed hard at her as he walked closer trying to determine if this girl could really be that beautiful princess he had danced with at the balls. His eyes widened as he exclaimed, "You are, Ella! There is no mistaking your eyes."

She lowered her gaze, but he lifted her chin back up. "Why did you run away both nights?"

"I had to have the borrowed items back by midnight. Prince Royal, please believe me, I did not mean any harm and I—"

"Silence, you do not have to explain anything. Of course I understand, Ella. Do you even know why I was searching for you?"

"I can only guess."

"Then guess."

"I thought it to be— well because you— do you like me truly?" she had such a pleading look in her eyes that Royal's heart nearly broke from pity at the sight.

"Very, very much, Ella!" he assured her. "My parents had the ball only for me to find a bride. And I have. You. That is of course if you will have me?"

Cinderella was speechless! The prince wanted to marry her, even after he knew she was not nobility!

"But she's a commoner." Eric said, stating Cinderella's thoughts.

"So. I am the prince and I can choose who I want. Besides my parents would not have allowed commoners to attend if they were against the thought of my picking one of them."

Cinderella glanced bashfully at the prince and replied in a soft voice, "If you truly wish it, my Prince, so be it."

"It is exactly what I wish. Of course I will go and ask your parents' permission as well. You don't think they will say no to me do you?"

Cinderella laughed, "They would have no reason to!"

"Splendid! Now we must go and let my parents know that you have been found!"

Cinderella gasped, she had forgotten about his mother. She would never allow the marriage.

Royal offered Cinderella his arm and escorted her to the throne room where his parents were presiding over matters of state.

"Mother, Father! I have found Ella! She has agreed to marry me."

"That is wonder—" the words died on Octavia's lips when she saw Cinderella. "Her?! She is a commoner! A servant! A scullery maid!" the queen rose from her throne in a rage.

"Her name is Ella and she is to be my wife."

"Son? This looks nothing like the princess that you danced with." his father said hesitantly.

"She isn't a princess, Father, and she never was. She says that she is Ella, and I know she is telling the truth. Clean her up and give her a fancy gown and you will see it's the truth. Please, Father she is the one, and the only one for me!"

"No! I forbid it! She is not nobility! You cannot marry anyone so lowly! You far outrank her my son." the queen argued.

"Mother. I have decided." Royal was firm on the matter and in the end his parents had to consent. After all there was no law forbidding such a match.

Royal had his carriage made ready and escorted Ella to her home.

The Hodgesheds were eaten up with jealousy when they saw and heard of the news of the engagement. Cinderella's parents were shocked but completely elated for the good fortune to their beloved daughter. To marry the prince was beyond anything they had ever imagined possible for her. And of course, they would never say no to such a match.

The wedding was arranged to be held in one week, and Cinderella felt like she could never be happier. Everything was happening so quickly, and she felt lost in a fairy tale.

Chapter 6

Queen Octavia was in a rage. She absolutely refused to let her son marry that girl! She could not and would not allow it. She thought and thought of a way to remove Cinderella from the kingdom and her son's life – forever. But the king was useless in this matter. He was happy that his son had found someone that he wanted to marry. The girl seemed nice enough and since there were no laws forbidding the marriage. He tried to encourage her to be happy for their child. At least the boy was going to settle down and they wouldn't have to worry about him going sailing all the time.

No, if there was anything to be done, she was going to have to be the one to take care of it, no one else would be able to help.

"Forrest. I've always been able to rely on you." the queen was meeting in secret with her most faithful servant. She had always been able to count on him to do any deeds that required secrecy. Normally, it was only to surprise her husband or son in little matters, but she knew she could rely on him in this as well.

"Yes, Your Highness." he bowed low.

"I need to get rid of the girl, Cinderella. She is not worthy to marry my son, and— well, I suppose I do have a personal grudge against her. She has to go away. Forever."

He bowed again, though she could see the uncertainty in his eyes.

"It is the best for the kingdom and my son." she reassured him. "It is a simple matter. Take this and deposit it amongst her things. Drop it in her pocket or something like that. It is just a few pieces of my jewelry. Tomorrow I will raise the cry that they are missing. The servants, and everyone else at the palace, will be detained, questioned, and searched. When the pouch is found on her person, she will be accused, and banished."

"Theft, of this kind, is normally punished by death." he commented.

"She will receive banishment in honor of my son's love for her. A kinder way to remove her. I'm not that cruel that I would have her killed for a false theft."

Forrest bowed and took the satchel from the queen. He concealed it amongst his person and left the chamber. He was still unsure of the matter but he dared not disobey the queen.

Octavia nodded to herself and wiped her hands on her silk skirt. "So it must be." she muttered.

ଔ

"Come along, Ella." Royal and Ella were walking through the garden, but she had paused to admire some flowers. Never had she seen such a variety of flowers anywhere in the kingdom. She was entranced by all the colors and various shapes of the blooms.

"Roy." she blushed, she still felt awkward calling him by his first name but he insisted that she should, "if you cannot stop to appreciate the beauty of flowers, then what else don't you appreciate?"

"It's not a matter of me not appreciating it. I've just seen it all my entire life, and when I want to show you something then I don't wish to stop. Oh just come on!"

Ella followed without stopping him anymore, but she knew she would have to come back sometime so she could enjoy the garden fully. He led her through the twisting paths till they reached a rose bower. He paused and breathed in the scent of the roses.

"This is beautiful!" Ella breathed in wonder.

"It's my favorite place in the gardens. Mother often brought me here when I was a child." he replied.

They sat in the shade of the bushes for a few minutes and Ella realized there were both red, white, and pink blooms weaving their way up the trellis.

The wandered around some more, talking and sharing stories of their lives, though Ella realized that he talked the most and didn't seem all that interested in hearing about her life.

They eventually returned inside and a servant girl met them. "Your ladyship, Ella." she curtsied and continued, "Her Majesty, Queen Octavia wishes to speak with you privately."

Ella was nervous, but she followed the servant girl to the queen's chambers. The door was shut behind her as she entered and Ella walked over to the queen who was sitting on a settee by the window.

"Ella! I'm glad you came. I just wished to apologize for that silly grudge I've been holding against you. It's ridiculous to think that I could stay mad at you for so long, and just for a silly grape pudding! It was foolish of me and I wish to say I am sorry. You seem like such a wonderful girl, and Royal is quite taken with you."

Cinderella was surprised and yet confused, but she sank into a curtsey and said, "Thank you."

"No hard feelings— daughter?"

"Oh, none!" Cinderella smiled and the queen smiled back.

"I have something I want to give you." Octavia said. She opened a fancy wooden jewelry box and pulled out a simple silver chain with an emerald in the center. "This was a necklace that my mother gave to me to wear on my wedding day, and I wish for you to have it as well. To carry on the tradition so to speak."

"Oh, but I couldn't! I mean it's so lovely—"

"Please. If there is to be nothing between us, dear girl. Take it as a token of good will if nothing more."

Ella slowly took the offered necklace and replied quietly, "Thank you, Your Majesty."

At that moment, a knock sounded on the door, the queen called out a curt "Come in." and the servant girl entered followed closely by the queen's servant, Forrest. He walked over to the queen and handed her a letter with a stiff bow.

"Thank you. You may go." she said with a wave of her hand. Forrest turned to go, and "accidentally" bumped into

Cinderella. As he did, he slipped the small pouch of jewels into her front pocket. He left the room and the queen broke the seal on the letter. She glanced at it and rose abruptly from her seat, "Excuse me a moment, dear." she left the room to find the servant girl so that she could deliver a reply and once more returned to her seat on the settee.

"That was really all that I wanted to say, Ella. I am so looking forward to having you here as my daughter-in-law."

Cinderella smiled and curtsied. Thanking the queen again, she left the room. Perhaps the queen had really decided to put her grudge aside. Ella was always willing to give someone a second chance and believe for the best in a person.

Not twenty-minutes after her meeting with the queen did a screech ring through the castle. Word was soon out that the queen's diamond necklace and bracelet were missing. Everyone was to be detained, questioned, and searched. Royal was there with his parents watching the proceedings and Ella was right beside him. She tried to think of who could be responsible for the outrage of stealing from the queen.

Every servant, guard, and anybody else that was at the palace at the time was searched, but without any result. Once the proceedings were done the royal family was left alone.

"My dear, was there no one else? Any guests that may have left before you noticed them missing?" the king asked in confusion.

"No, the jewels were there with me. I had Ella in my room and gave her the emerald necklace. You know the one I got from my mother. It was after that I found them gone. I—wait! Ella was alone in my room when Forrest brought me the message from the Duchess Lori! I left for just a moment and then…" she trailed off with a shrug of her shoulders.

"Mother! You are not implying that Ella stole your jewels are you?!" Royal stepped forward indignantly.

"Well, everyone else was questioned and searched…"

"What would be the point of her stealing anything? We are to be married, she would have more jewels than she could ever hope to own in a lifetime!"

"To give to her parents? How should I know!"

"Son, Octavia, silence! Please. Ella, child, did you see the necklace and bracelet when my wife gave you the gift? Or perhaps was there anyone else in the room when she left"

Ella was terrified, how could she be blamed for this crime? But she spoke out calmly, "I cannot say either way, Your Highness. There were many jewels in the box. I did not pay close attention. When I was alone I stood where I had been and did not open the box. I did not steal anything, nor did I see anyone else enter the room before, Her Majesty's return."

"There you are! Satisfied, Mother?!"

"No, she has to be searched as everyone else was."

"Mother!"

"Son, if it relieves your mother's mind, there is no harm." the king interjected. "Besides what harm is there is the girl is truly innocent."

Octavia called for one of her handmaidens to come and take Cinderella away to have her searched as everyone else had been.

They came back in only a moment, Cinderella was ghastly white and the handmaiden was clutching a bag.

"This was in her pocket." she said handing it to the queen with a sad, confused backwards glance at Ella.

Octavia opened it and out fell the necklace and bracelet. A gasp escaped everyone's throats.

Royal stared at Ella. A tear slipped down her cheek, "I didn't do it!" she said hoarsely.

There was deathly silence and then the king spoke in a strained voice. "Ella, you do know what the punishment of stealing is, don't you?"

Ella swallowed and choked, "Yes."

"Wait!" Octavia interrupted, "You cannot execute her, my husband."

Royal sighed in relief, but it was too soon.

"Banish her instead. I cannot see the girl that my son loves so much – killed."

"Then so it shall be. Cinderella, you shall be banished to Isla Prehendere for the theft of jewels from Queen Octavia."

"NO!" Royal yelled.

"I didn't do it!" Ella gasped. But already guards were taking her away. Royal sprang down to try to wrest her from them, but his father's voice commanded, "Royal, I have spoken. Banishment is her allotment and you shall not interfere."

Royal stumbled back. Blinded by his own tears he raced from the room and found Eric. He told his friend the entire tale. No one noticed the satisfied look on Octavia's smug face as Ella was dragged to the dungeon where she would stay till she was conducted to the ship which would take her to the Isle.

Chapter 7

Mist hung over the city as a cart rumbled through the streets carrying a solitary person. Cinderella was to be put aboard the ship which would take her to Isla Prehendere, the prison Isle. She was the only prisoner to be banished at this time. She was terrified out of her wits. Her clothes and hair were unkempt and she looked a sorry sight. She hadn't seen Royal since that day in the throne room which was three days ago. She had also not heard if her parents had been told the news of her banishment. Tear marks lined her cheeks and more threatened to spill over as she saw the masts of the ship which would take her away from all that she loved.

The guards, rather kindly, helped her down from the cart and led her to the ship. The captain looked sorrowfully at her, then ordered his men back to the barracks once the captain of the ship had charge of Cinderella. She was put into the hold where the prisoners were normally kept.

After an hour they were out to sea. The ship's captain felt sorry for Cinderella and allowed her to come up to the deck, free of any bonds. After all, what could a girl do to a group of hardened seamen? Since she was the only prisoner he couldn't be accused of favoritism either.

Cinderella leaned over the railing feeling the cool, sea breeze blow into her face. Under different circumstances she would have enjoyed being out there on the ocean she had always wondered what it would be like, but right now it only held sorrow for her and she could not enjoy the beauty of the open seas. Some tears fell down her face and she didn't even bother to brush them aside.

"Hullo." a voice said behind her.

Cinderella turned and saw a tall, young man watching her. He was dressed in sailor's clothes and was very tanned and muscular. His medium length, blonde hair blew around his nicely featured face. He had very melancholy grey eyes which crinkled at the corners when he smiled but also made him look perpetually sad.

She turned her attention back to the sea but replied with a quiet, "Hello."

"I'm William. You?" he leaned against the railing beside her as he studied her face.

"Cinderella." she didn't feel like talking, but she also didn't want to be rude to the young man who seemed nice enough from her first impression.

"Nice to meet you. If there is anything that I can do for you do not hesitate to ask. You don't need to feel like you are a prisoner aboard this ship."

Cinderella gave him a half-smile and said, "Thank you, William. It is very kind of you."

"WILLIAM!" a voice bellowed from across the deck. They both turned and saw the captain of the ship approaching them.

"Yes, Sir?"

"Boy, there is plenty to be doing instead of loitering with the girl."

Will blushed as he walked away with a goodbye to Cinderella.

"He's a good, lad." the captain commented after William had left. "We will do all we can to make this voyage as comfortable for you as possible."

"You are too kind." Cinderella said thanking him.

"Nonsense. You are the first female… uh… prisoner that we've had in a long time. We don't want to make this time for you any more difficult than it is."

"You are very considerate. Thank you, Captain."

"My pleasure. And what's your name, child?"

"Pardon, it's Cinderella."

"I'm pleased to meet you, Cinderella. Feel free to call me Captain Vincent." he then walked away letting her be by herself.

The days passed slowly for Cinderella at first, but once she became more comfortable with the sailors, and especially the friendship that started growing with William, she was fascinated by everything that they did aboard the ship. William showed her everything and tried to explain how it all functioned.

"How long will it take to reach the Isle?" she asked one night when they were out on deck watching the stars.

"With the steady wind and the good weather we've been having, also if it stays like this, then we can make it in a month."

"Then that means that there is only about three weeks left."

"About, maybe more though."

"Will? Have you been to the Isle before?"

"A few times. No other ship will take me on because they think me too young and inexperienced. This is the only one that would give me a chance. Since I love the sea so much, I would rather be aboard this ship than none at all. But it is definitely not the ship of anyone's choice. Guarding prisoners, having to visit the Isle, and not being able to be out to sea quite as much as a sailor would like."

"Maybe one day you'll be able to move to another ship."

"I hope so… but you never know. Something would have to happen to change the course of my future, and it'd have to be something very big."

"What's the island like?" fear had crept into her voice and Will could see the nervous light in her eyes. He wasn't sure how to answer her.

"Well…" he started slowly. "It *is* a prison. There's a large fortress with guards around the entire Isle. There's no ship stationed there so no one can escape. Everyone lives in a community type environment. You can even have your own homes, gardens, and basically everything you could need. I know some people that have set up there own types of businesses."

"Are any of the prisoners ever mean? Or have any of them hurt someone?"

"You mean, is it safe?"

"Yes."

"Sure, as I said there are guards that watch over everyone. I do know that some prisoners have had to be put in isolation. But it is not common and you never get told why they can't be with the others. Most everyone gets along fine."

"Can you ever leave?" Cinderella asked in a very quiet voice.

"In a rare occasion you may be pardoned. But that is very rare."

"Do you know why I was banished?"

"I heard the story. We always do. You were found with the queen's diamond necklace and bracelet and you supposedly stole them."

"I didn't." she stated in a small voice.

"What can you say when the evidence is against you."

"Will, I don't know how, but I never stole! Think of the reasoning! There is none to support theft on my part! Royal would have given me anything I could have desired! I had no need to steal his mother's jewels."

"True, it does seem strange. There were ideas circulating as to possible motives."

"What are they? Tell me, please."

"People thought that you were using the prince to gain access to the palace, steal anything you needed or wanted, and then disappear before the wedding."

"I would never have! I wanted to marry the prince! Besides I already had some access since I was a scullery maid there."

"Of course, but that's just what some people are saying."

"If only there were a way to show my innocence." she practically whispered.

"Well, if there is ever any way that I can help prove it I am completely at your service."

"Thank you, Will. Your belief in me is greatly appreciated. As well as your friendship."

William smiled and turned his gaze to the sea. They stood there for awhile before Cinderella went to her room and to bed. Will watched her go with a sad expression on his face.

"I swear to help you, Cinders." he murmured to himself.

Chapter 8

No ill weather had come to hinder the progress of the ship, and they were now halfway to Isla Prehendere. With every passing day, Cinderella's fear and unease grew. The only thing she could count on was the strong friendship that had come between her and William. He listened to everything she said. She had told him all about herself, her early life in the bakery with her parents; then the fateful day of the first proclamation; how she had met the old woman and the borrowed the dresses; dancing with the prince and his notice to find her; and finally the engagement to Royal and her accusation of crimes and subsequent banishment.

Will believed she was innocent and was very sorry for her. He greatly liked Cinders and having her aboard ship made this voyage the best he had ever had. There was no one else around his age and he enjoyed her company and friendship. He told her his story. How he had grown up near the docks and had always been fascinated and drawn to the sea. His father had been a sailor, until an encounter with pirates had cost him his leg and he was dismissed from the crew. William became a cabin boy on a small ship when he was eight and from then had never been without a ship to sail on. Because he had not been on the ship as the cabin boy very long before the captain had died, he was not thought to have gained enough experience to serve anywhere else than the prison ship. No one ever wanted to be part of that crew and every sailor left whenever the opening aboard another ship came up.

Cinderella wished that her new friend would be able to get on a new ship, but it seemed unlikely anytime soon.

The other sailors aboard the ship liked Cinderella as well. She was a merry spirit amongst them, even though it was she that would have to remain on the Isle. They all felt sorry for her, and none truly thought that she was guilty. She talked the cook into letting her make the sailors some treats that she would have made with her parents in the bakery, and from that day on she was always helping the cook, either teaching him new recipes, or making something special to surprise the crew with.

One evening, the crew had gathered about while the musicians played some tunes to liven up the night and lift the men's spirits.

"Come on, Cinderella! Dance with me!" one of the crew called to her.

She was sitting near the flutist and only shook her head, smiling at the sailor.

"You're too old, Henri!" A man called out jovially, "Anyone can tell that she wouldn't want to dance with someone that won't be able to keep up with the music! Besides, she would need a partner closer to her own age."

"I doubt that's true! And I can dance just fine! I'm sure she would dance with me!" another crewman spoke up.

"Then ask her and see!"

"Well… Miss, would you care to dance?"

"No, thank you!" Cinderella replied with a smile. "I prefer to sit and listen, but any of you can dance by yourselves! I'm sure that would be entertaining for all."

"Oh, come boys, you know she'll refuse all of you!" Captain Vincent said.

"Why?"

"Because William is the only one of this here crew that could ever hope of having her say yes to such a request."

"Not true!" William said.

The rest of the crew sided with the captain. "Go on and ask her and prove it then, Will! Everyone can tell that you're sweet on her! And I think she may be a bit on you!"

William colored slightly, but he was so sure that she wouldn't that he did get up and crossed the deck to her. With a bow that looked far out of place on the ship, he said, "Cinders, would you honor me with a dance."

Cinderella laughed and climbed to her feet, taking Will's hand she said, "It would be my honor." The embarrassment it was causing him was too much to pass up on.

Will turned even redder, but he led her into the lively dance that Cinderella had watched many times. The other crew tapped in time to the fiddler.

"What did I tell you!" the captain hooted while the others laughed and clapped.

Finally the dance was over, Cinderella was quite winded and flushed, yet still smiled happily. William stood panting somewhat from the exertion of the dance, and his blonde hair flopped messily about his face.

"Thank you very much, dear Cinders." he said overly gallant while bowing again.

She curtsied her best curtsey and replied, "Twas a pleasure, Sir."

They both laughed along with the crew. Soon Cinderella retired, very worn out from the dance, but very happy. As she fell asleep she thought to herself that it wouldn't be so bad to stay like this forever. As long as she could forget about all that she had lost.

Chapter 9

"Cinders?" William greeted her the next morning with a smile and question.

"Good-morning, Will. What is it?" she asked noticing a strange look in his eyes.

"Me and the lads were talking last night, after you went to bed. And— well— they all thought of something. They want you to stay aboard the ship, with us, as part of the crew— like the cook's help. We would never even have to hand you over to the guards on the Isle. No one would know for we would never tell them… but— well—"

"Will." Cinders interrupted, "I could never do that! I thank everyone for their kindness for wanting me to stay, but I would not be able to live in secrecy. What if one day someone saw me that knew me, or word got out that I had never arrived at the Isle. Everyone would be in such horrible trouble! I could never bring that on anyone! No, William, I must go to Isla Prehendere and stay there until the day I die or if I am found innocent."

"That is what I thought you would say. I was singled out to ask you, but I understand and I wouldn't want you to agree to something that would make you unhappy. But also know, the Isle isn't expecting you. They never get word of new prisoners arriving. And the kingdom doesn't really follow up with them too well."

Cinderella smiled at her friend and replied, "Will, I know it is just because you are all my friends. But just take me there and leave me, it will be best for all. Besides, I'm sure they will be asking if I arrived…"

No more was spoken of the crew's idea, but all heard of her reply. They were disappointed, especially the cook, but they agreed with her decision and allowed it to be as she wished.

The days continued to pass with fine weather and they steadily drew ever closer to the Isle.

One day, sails appeared on the horizon. The ship steadily drew nearer and nearer. Finally they could make out the flag— black with a skull and crossed sword.

"Pirates."

"Will they attack us?" Cinders asked Will.

"Yes, anyway they'll board us. They've done so in the past to take the prisoners and press-gang them into service on their ship. Usually it is after they've lost a considerable amount of men, but since you are our only prisoner— well…" he trailed off with a shrug of his broad shoulders.

"They won't take me, surely!" Cinderella's eyes were wide in fear at the thought.

"I don't know… you can never guess what a pirate will do!"

The ship drew closer still, and before long the report of a cannon echoed across the waters. The shot fell far short of the ship.

"Only a warning. They want us to surrender before a fight." Will explained.

"Will we?"

William glanced at the captain who was standing near the ship's wheel. "More than likely. It could save our lives and the ship."

By late afternoon, the two ships were not very far apart. The sailors could see the pirates milling around on their deck now.

"Cinders! Go to the hold and stay there!" William ordered.

"No, not the hold." the captain had come up behind them. "They'll search there for sure. Go to my cabin, Cinderella."

Cinderella did as he told her, and the pirates soon boarded the ship.

"Ah, tis a pleasure to be doin' business with ye again." the pirate captain addressed Captain Vincent as soon as he boarded.

"We aren't doing any business with you. It would be best if you just re-boarded your own vessel and left."

"But me and me mates are needin' some new members to the crew. You're just the ship to ask for help."

"We have no one that can be of service to you."

"Ah, then what be ye carryin' this time if not prisoners."

"We are not carrying anything of worth to pirates."

I'll be the judge o' that. Starling, search the ship!" the pirate captain commanded

The man called Starling was standing behind the captain and was apparently the bosun. As soon as his captain called upon him he ordered other men to search the hold while he went to help search other areas of the ship, the captain's cabin especially. He had long black hair tied in a ponytail and a pale, jagged scar ran across his left cheek. He was very tall and muscular but not overly so. His eyes were dark brown and lined in kohl to protect them from the glare of the sunlight. Gold hoop earrings dangled from his ears, a large medallion hung round his neck, and expensive rings were on his fingers. His skin was deeply tanned. His features were very fine, almost delicate, but he also had a firmness about him that caused everyone that came in contact with him to respect and obey him. He was deadly with his cutlass and was a perfect shot with his pistols, there was no better fighter in the pirate crew than him. Two large, leather belts hung about his waist. Another belt hung across his chest with shot for his pistols and was also where he carried the weapons.

He crossed the deck in a few long strides and immediately kicked the door open. Captain Vincent placed a restraining hand on William's arm for the young man nearly stormed across the deck after Starling. William glanced at his captain who shook his head in silence. Perhaps Cinders had some sense about her. No sound came from the cabin, but the rest of the pirate crew could be heard in the hold.

Ever so slowly the crew came back to their captain, a few had some nearly worthless baubles, gunpowder, or other food supplies, but nothing of great worth or importance. Starling still had not returned.

"You know, Cap'n. I am curious as to why someone like you would be out on the seas without any prisoners." the pirate spoke up.

Captain Vincent turned his attention back to the pirate captain. "Captain Albatross, I have no prisoners aboard this ship. The only prisoner that we were taking to the Isle was an older man that became quite ill. We gave him a burial yesterday. We're so close to the Isle we thought we would stop off there to let them know and give the crew a rest before heading back to port."

"A likely story." a firm voice said behind the them. Vincent turned and saw Starling standing there. His hand was clasped firmly on Cinderella's arm and a deathly look was in his eyes.

Chapter 10

"She isn't a prisoner!" Captain Vincent exclaimed. "She's-she's the cook's—"

"Enough! She's told me who she is! Am I to believe her or you? Why would an innocent person lie that she was a prisoner?" Starling butted in.

Vincent's face paled ever so slightly and he glanced at Cinderella. She stared straight ahead, only the nearly imperceptible clenching of her jaw showed any emotion.

Starling roughly pushed Cinderella forward and led the way back towards the pirate ship.

"Stop! Wait! You can't take her!" a voice yelled out. It was William.

Starling stopped and, without releasing his tight grip on Cinders' arm, turned slightly to face William. "I can." he said in a quiet voice.

"No! There is no need! She's of no use on a pirate ship!"

Starling glanced at Cinderella and then looked back at William, "There are uses for her." he shoved her on.

The rest of the crew had already boarded their ship taking what they had found. The captain turned to go as well. When their backs were to them, William tried once more,

"STOP!" he hollered.

Captain Vincent tried to grab hold of him, there was nothing any of them could do to help Cinderella now, but William evaded the grip and drew his sword.

Starling instantly shoved Cinderella forward, causing her to stumble and nearly fall off the plank between the ships. The pirate captain was the only thing that saved her from going overboard. Starling had his own sword out of its scabbard and parried William's blow.

"Only a coward tries to attack from the back." he growled through gritted teeth. William was no match to the experienced pirate and he was soon shoved back to his crew.

"Be glad I promised her I would spare all of your lives or you would be dead right now." Starling hissed when William's sword clattered to the deck. Swiftly, Starling turned on his heel and was back on his ship before any of them had moved.

☙

"Ye do not need to be frightened, child." Cinderella was in the pirate captain's cabin. He was sitting at his desk and Cinderella stood before him. Starling stood slightly behind her with a hand resting lightly on the hilt of his cutlass.

Cinderella looked at the captain. He seemed like he could be a nice man. His hair was bright red as was his beard. His eyes were a soft grey. He was on the shorter side, not nearly as tall as Starling. He wore elaborate clothes made of the finest cloth of silks and velvets of a myriad colors. Rings bedecked his fingers and many necklaces hung from his neck. His cabin was perfectly clean; the bed made, the table scrubbed, the book cases that were crammed full were entirely dusted, the tea set on the table was spotless.

"I am not afraid." Cinderella spoke up, even though her voice wavered slightly from a tremor of nervousness.

"Tell me your name."

"Cinderella."

"Well, child, I am Cap'n Albatross. That there is Starling, me bosun and son."

Cinderella immediately glanced at the tall, silent man. He stared unashamedly back at her. Cinderella could see no likeness between Captain Albatross and his boatswain.

"I know the family resemblance isn't very deep. Now tell me, Starling why did ye bring her along?" a hint of impatience was in his voice.

Starling stepped forward and said, "She's a prisoner. She told me her story and she offered her life in exchange for leaving the rest of the crew. I accepted, besides she can cook."

"Did ye say 'cook'?"

"Aye, Cap'n."

"Ye can cook, girl?" he turned back to addressing Cinderella.

"Yes, Sir."

"Ah… that's a mighty good thing then." she couldn't tell if he meant for her or for his son. "See our cook died and we've been makin' do ever since." Captain Albatross paused a moment as if thinking. "Starling. Show Miss Cinderella her new quarters."

"Aye-aye, Cap'n." Starling responded. "Come on." he said turning to her.

She followed passively and Starling led her swiftly across deck and to the hold where she was installed at the cook's station. The rest of the day was spent cooking for the crew. And the next morning, afternoon, evening, and on and on and on. Days passed in a blur, it felt like she was always cooking.

Some of the pirates would loiter about and talk to her. It wasn't long before all of them knew about her engagement to Prince Royal and her banishment upon the accusation of theft. Some seemed to believe her innocent, the captain and Starling did, but others thought that she did do it and it proved her to be one of them.

Cinderella soon got into the custom of getting up, cooking, cleaning, cooking, cleaning, cooking, cleaning, watching the sunset and finally going to bed just to start all over. She never saw the captain, except to give him his meals, and she hardly ever saw Starling. There was no other ships spotted and so, thankfully for Cinderella, there were no sea battles. The weather also stayed very fine.

One of the pirates had taken a liking to Cinderella and soon would not leave her be. He would constantly be sitting nearby watching her cook and clean and asking for taste-tests. Cinderella grew tired of him and wished that he would stay away. If she asked him to go he would laugh, showing his ugly yellow, gappy teeth.

One evening, after the supper had been consumed, Cinderella was cleaning up the mess before going up to get some fresh air and watching the sunset. As she was doing her work, the pirate came down to watch her, instead of sitting in his customary corner, he pulled a crate closer to where she was working and sat down.

"You know, Cinderella, we'll be landin' in port in a few days. Once we do, we'll get land leave. While there, you could comes with me and we could get married all proper like."

Cinderella nearly choked, as it was she couldn't say anything for a moment. Finally she managed, "I do not want to marry you."

"Come now, I'd be a good man to ye!" he stood up and walked uncomfortably close to her side.

"I said no." she replied trying to quickly finish so she could leave to the deck where the other pirates would be.

"I know I can help ye change your mind." the man whispered in his rough voice. She could smell his rummy odor and feel his thick, hot breath on her neck. She tried to move away, but he dogged her steps.

"Please excuse me. I already—"

"She said *no*." an icily cold voice spoke behind them.

The pirate turned and Starling stepped into the dim light.

"Get out of here…" Starling trailed off leaving a threat hanging over their heads. The pirate knew better than to cross Starling and he quickly hopped out of the room.

"How long?" Starling asked.

"I'm sorry?"

"How long has he been bothering you."

"Oh… well, I don't know. I mean he's only been like that today, but he sits around here all the time. I can't say when it started." Cinderella stammered averting her gaze from the cold stare of the young man.

"How many other men have been bothering you?"

"None."

"Yet…" Starling trailed off looking about the cramped cooking quarters.

Cinderella didn't reply.

"I came to tell you, Cap'n Albatross wants ye in his cabin. Now."

Cinderella followed as Starling led her into the captain's quarters.

"I've been payin' close attention to ye, Cinderella. You're a good lass. Starling though is concerned that you're ailing. Are ye?"

"Ailing, Sir?"

"Aye, sick girl!"

"Oh— well, nothing to note, Sir."

"You do look a might paler than afore."

"I've been below deck most times during the day. I'm just not getting as much sun as before. I'm sure that is all it is."

"That not be too good for ye, I think. Starling also has expressed concern that some o' the crew may not be treatin' you in proper ways that a lady should be. Is that true?"

Cinderella glanced at Starling's blank face and wondered how much he had heard and seen previously, she had never noticed him anywhere nearby. She replied slowly, "Only one has bothered me in any way, Captain."

"One can soon be more. What I have decided on is this: once we reach port, we'll be resupplying, I'll get a new ship's cook so it will relieve you of those duties. You'll be able to be above deck where you can get your sunlight, and where Starling and I can keep an eye on ye."

"Thank you, Captain. But may I ask what good am I aboard this vessel if I am no longer cook? Are you taking me somewhere?"

"Girl, do ye want to live on Isla Prehendere?"

"Not exactly."

"If we were to put you off anywhere and they found out about ye, they'd have ye shipped directly there. We be doin' ye a favor, girl! No, you're best chance is to throw in your lot with the rest o' us."

"But I don't want to be a pirate!" she bit her lip in apprehension. She hadn't meant to say that aloud.

"You're our captive." Starling finally spoke. "You cannot leave. We don't want you to be cook anymore since it is too tiring of a job for you. I've noticed. Being below deck is not where most of us are – anyway the trustworthy ones – so it is not the safest place for a young woman to be by herself. We are doing this for your health and protection. You can teach the cook new recipes. Help him if need be, and I'm sure there will be other uses for you later."

Starling wasn't all that clear and Cinderella tried to guess what 'other uses' there could possibly be for her! But she just replied in a puzzled tone, "Thank you for caring so much for my well being."

Starling bowed slightly. Cinderella was suddenly struck with a strange sense of knowing someone like him before. Back at home. But who he reminded her of she could not say.

"Cinderella. You'll be bunking in Starling's cabin from now on." Cap'n Albatross announced.

Cinderella's eyes grew wide in shock and she turned scarlet,"But-but, Captain— I— that— what I mean—"

A merry laugh behind her pulled her up short in her stuttering. She turned to Starling who was the one laughing. She had never heard him laugh, but he had quite a nice sounding laugh and she liked it.

"Cinderella, if you think that my father is saying that you and I shall be sharing a cabin, you are dreadfully mistaken! I will be moving in here with my father so that we may be near by if you have need of me and also you will have a much better place to stay at and the privacy a lady deserves."

Cinderella breathed a sigh of relief and said, "Thank you both. It is very kind of you."

"Nonsense. We took you aboard, and so we should treat a lady a little more civilly. No one will be able to blame us of not being gentlemen!" Captain Albatross put in.

Cinderella turned back to him and he had a bemused smile about his lips. Probably from Cinderella's misunderstanding.

"One other thing, you may help yourself to the lot of me books. There is a fine collection here and I'm sure it will help pass the time for ye."

"Thank you, Captain." she turned back around and said, "And thank you… Starling."

Starling nodded his head, "You are most welcome. I am entirely at your service. Feel free to come to me with anything that you may need." Then he turned smartly on his heel and strode out the door to attend to his men.

"Starling's a good lad. He'll always do right by any of us."

"Captain, may I ask you something?" with Starling's presence gone, Cinderella felt a little braver in the presence of the jovial captain. Starling always made her tongue feel tied in knots and her thoughts jumbled.

"Anything, me dear!"

"Well, Captain why are you *truly* doing this for me? I mean why would it matter if I was taken to Isla Prehendere? What concern is it of yours what becomes of me?"

"We took ye, girl. That is what matters."

"But if I am of no use to you now?"

"Starling has plans for ye."

"But—"

"Enough, child!" he laughed as he held a hand up to stop her chatter, "Think of me as a father that doesn't want anything bad to happen to his beautiful, innocent daughter. I know ye don't belong on the Isle! I know ye are a good girl that was accused wrongly. We don't want anything bad to happen to ye now. And since we took ye prisoner that makes us responsible for ye. Now enough talk of all this. Go on and enjoy the rest o' the night. Starling will show ye to the cabin."

Cinderella thanked the captain again and left the cabin. The sun had set by the time she got to deck. There was only a faint red glow that still tinged the quickly darkening sky.

"Cinderella?"

She turned and found Starling behind her. He was leaning against the captain's cabin waiting for her. She smiled slightly and waited for him to speak.

"If you're ready, I can show you your new quarters."

"Yes, thank you." she replied as she followed him across the deck to his separate cabin. Inside was a ordinary looking ship cabin. There was a bunk, a small table, charts on the walls, a seaman's trunk, and a couple chairs. But what surprised Cinderella was the decorations. Hung from the ceiling, lining the room, and in every nook and cranny there were seashells of all shapes, colors, and size. Some were strung together on long cords, others were just sitting on any available space.

"You collect shells?" Cinderella asked in amazement. Never had she seen so many, or such pretty ones.

"Yes. They remind me of the islands and other lands that I've visited." he answered a tad smug.

"They're beautiful." she said smiling up at him with her eyes.

He half smiled in reply, "Good then, I have no fear that you will break any of them."

"Of course not!"

"Well I shall be in the captain's cabin if you need anything. Do not hesitate to ask." he bowed rather stiffly and was about to leave when Cinderella asked,

"Starling… um when do we make port?"

"Five more days most likely. We should start seeing land in probably the next day or two."

"Then am I allowed on shore?"

"Do you want to go?"

"I would like it very much!"

"Then I will take you with me. It will be safest that way."

Starling turned again to leave and Cinderella called after him, "Thank you."

Chapter 11

"It's been over a month now! She's for sure on the Isle by now! Eric, I cannot live knowing that she's there in that accursed place! And accused so wrongfully! What am I to do?!"

Prince Royal was pacing about his room like a caged tiger. Ever since Ella's banishment he had been doing everything in his power to reverse her sentence. After it was entirely clear that his father would never change his mind, Royal put all of his efforts into finding out the real culprit. He believed Ella entirely innocent and refused to allow her to be put away on Isla Prehendere without a proper fight from him. But no evidence was ever found as to who else could have framed his darling Ella for the hideous deed.

His parents started to worry about him. He was not the same son that they had cared for and loved his entire life. His joy and spirit were gone. He could be heard far into the night pacing about his room and muttering to himself like a madman. His hair and clothes were always unkempt. Even the fine weather they were having did not entice him to go out to sea, which this time would have made his parents quite happy. He wouldn't speak to his parents except to respond to a question with a monosyllabic answer if he deemed it necessary. Eric was the only one that he would actually talk to, and the only one that he would allow in his presence anymore.

Eric was at a loss of what to do for his prince and friend. He knew that he should try to dissuade Roy from putting all his energy into a futile case, but as his friend he could not do so knowing that Royal seemed to truly love Ella. Besides, Eric believed Ella was innocent as well and wished she would be cleared of the theft.

Together they questioned anyone and everyone that could have had any connection to the case, but his own mother never came to Royal's mind as a possibility. Ella had never told Royal about the queen's dislike of her, and Royal had no inkling that there could be any reason that his mother would begrudge Cinderella marrying him, other than the fact that she was a commoner. So Royal would pace his room, roam the gardens, stalk the castle all to no avail; and Eric followed like a dog and tried to attend to all the prince's needs.

"Royal, there's nothing either of us can do anymore! She's been sentenced and banished. I am afraid that is going to have to be the end of it!'

"Eric, you believe her innocent. You told me so."

"Yes."

"Why can't we make everyone else believe her innocent as well?! Who stole the jewels?"

"Maybe no one!"

"No one?"

"I mean… you know…"

"No, I don't. Someone had to steal them and leave them on Cinderella."

"Maybe the maid that searched her?"

"We questioned her. And it was apparently found in Ella's pocket, otherwise she would have said something about it not being in there."

"Unless..."

"Yes?!"

"Unless the maid had it stuck up her sleeve and she let it fall into Ella's pocket when she looked there."

"Not likely, Ella should have felt that, or— no, that doesn't seem plausible. Besides do you really want to blame *that* maid for the crime?" Royal looked at Eric who flushed slightly. The prince had apparently seen the way Eric and that particular maid were on quite friendly terms.

"Maybe she was employed by someone else to do it?" he asked confused.

"But that leaves the who!"

"Is there someone that would be jealous of her going to marry you? Someone that might want her gone so that she would have the chance to marry you once Ella was forgotten – not that it would be likely – but..."

"Eric! That's a wonderful thought! But who still? The princesses that had any chance are all gone and have been since the balls! It would have to be someone in the palace."

"Then I am still as lost as ever. I'm sorry, Royal. I am out of all and any ideas."

"I suppose we shall never clear her name then..."

Royal went into a depression that he hadn't yet experienced. The hopelessness of ever proving her innocent weighed heavily on his mind. He still couldn't sleep, he hardly ate, and now he didn't even talk to Eric! His parents worried about him and the doctor advised them to bring the girl back for him – thief or not – if she were married to him there would be no point in stealing anymore and everyone could keep a close eye on her. The king refused because of the queen's influence in the matter. She decided a ball might help get his mind off Ella and so introduce him, yet again, to a host of lovely, eligible, ladies. Ones that she had no grudge against.

All of this time Queen Octavia had never felt remorse for sending that scullery maid away to spend the rest of her life amongst true thieves, criminals, debtor prisoners, and other wrong-doers. She was only too happy to be rid of her. Nor did she look upon her son's health and obsession with clearing Ella's name as anything other than a passing phase in his life.

However, Forrest, the man that had carried out his queen's orders so perfectly, was feeling remorse. Cinderella was a good girl, he had known of her previously from when she was working in the kitchen, and he had seen her in her parent's bakery when he had been there to buy some bread. He had no ill feelings to her and he did feel sorry that so sweet a girl, and so innocent, should be sent to her doom because of a jealous queen. Of course it had to be jealousy, nothing else could spur a woman to commit such a crime against a poor girl. As he watched his prince's health and life decline, he felt strangely responsible for it and knew that if the prince died of a broken heart over Ella it would always lay on his conscious that it was his doing that had brought about the death of the heir to the kingdom.

The day before the ball, Forrest could no longer stand it. He walked silently to the prince's room that evening and knocked on the door. It was opened by Eric who gave him a questioning glance.

"Please, I have to speak to Prince Royal!" Forrest whispered, while glancing around making sure that no one had seen him.

"Royal is actually asleep. I do not wish to disturb him. Just tell me what you want and I will tell him when he awakens."

"No!" the man cried. "I must tell him now before I am missed! I have to tell him!"

"What is it about?"

"The girl – Cinderella – I have news. Please!"

At mention of Cinderella, Eric was all ears, "You know something about her?! What! Speak up, man!"

"The Prince." Forrest insisted. Eric hesitated, then let Forrest in and shut the door. Noiselessly he walked to Royal's bedside and gently shook him awake.

"Wha-who— Eric?" he mumbled as he sleepily sat up.

"Forrest – you know him – he has news about Cinderella."

"Ella!" the sleep vanished and Royal was immediately out of bed. He walked over to Forrest, "Tell me! What of Ella!"

Forrest lost his nerve. He buried his face in his hands and started to sob. Both men were confused, but Eric went and got a drink for Forrest. Once the older man had drunk and composed himself he began his story. He told all about the queen, what she asked him to do, when he did it, and he ended his tale. "I'm so sorry! I never thought about it hurting anyone! But the queen, she is not sorry in the least, and I-I couldn't live with myself anymore! I had to tell you! Please! I beg of thee to forgive me! I never wanted to do it but she is the queen and I did not know how to say no to her demand."

"You are forgiven." Roy stated laying a hand on the man's shoulder. "I thank you for bringing this news to me. Now I can clear Ella's name and she can come back and…" his voice trailed off and a bright light shone in his eyes. "I must tell Father!" he declared and strode from the room with Eric calling after him and Forrest entirely forgotten at the moment.

Neither of his parents were happy that they were awoken in the middle of the night, and they could not figure out what he was babbling about. Ella was innocent. There was proof. His mother… it was all just a jumble to them that meant nothing. Finally, Eric stepped forward and said,

"Excuse me, pardon me for interrupting, but perhaps I can tell you what Prince Royal is trying to say."

Royal agreed eagerly and Eric proceeded, "Prince Royal and I just heard a full confession of the person who did the crime. Meaning the supposed theft of Her Majesty's, Queen Octavia's, diamond bracelet and necklace. The items were never stolen. Queen Octavia was the one that gave them to the servant named Forrest with instructions to drop them in Ella's pocket and frame her for the theft. It all worked perfectly, and now Ella is banished falsely and—" but Eric was cut off by a strangled cry from the queen.

Everyone looked at her. She was deathly white and her eyes were large and full of fear and anger.

"Do you mean to imply that my wife, the queen, stole her own jewels to blame on this girl Ella?" the king asked.

"Not stole, Father. She just framed Ella for the crime. The jewels were given up of her own free will. Correct, Mother?" he snapped angrily.

But Octavia said nothing, she was shaking badly and suddenly, she fainted.

When she came to, they did get a full confession from her as well. Forrest was let go with no punishment, and Ella was pronounced innocent of any crime.

The ball was of course cancelled and Royal's ship was gotten ready for a voyage to take him to Isla Prehendere to bring back Ella so he could marry her and make her the princess of the entire Kingdom of Bleu Evine.

But if only he had known that she wasn't at the isle and was instead aboard a pirate ship with a person that would play a major part in everyone's lives very soon. A young man named Starling.

Chapter 12

The port they docked at was at a very strange looking land. Never had Cinderella seen such odd animals, plants, and people. The colors all seemed so much more vivid than anything she was previously used to. But it was all beautiful in a strangely exotic way.

"Are you ready?" Starling asked when they had docked and the other pirates were gladly taking leave to go waste their shares of the plunder that they had accumulated.

"Yes." she was now quite nervous to go on shore, but she didn't want Starling to see. He led her down the plank to the dock. As she stepped onto the solid ground, everything started reeling about and she felt quite dizzy. When she tried to walk, she felt herself falling. Instantly a strong arm was about her waist and she was held steady until everything quit moving about. She shook her head to clear it fully and looked up into Starling's face.

His expression was impossible to read, he stared back at her and opened his mouth to speak when she said, "I feel all right. You can let go now."

He took his arm slowly away, to make sure she was steady. Satisfied that she wasn't going to fall, he took off across the dock in his long, swift strides. Cinderella trotted behind trying to keep up. But it was not an easy task, she was soon panting and her legs and side were aching.

"Starling!" She gasped in as loud a voice as possible. She didn't think he would be able to hear, what with all the noise of the people on the docks and the distance that was between them. But he did hear her and he turned around. His eyes scanned over the crowd quickly till he spotted her and he walked back to where she had stopped to catch her breath.

"I'm sorry. I couldn't keep up." she panted when once again he was beside her. She couldn't tell if it was remorse in his face or if he had any feelings whatsoever about it. He shrugged his shoulders and waited another moment.

Once Cinderella was breathing steadily he said, "Come on. I'll try to take shorter steps."

"Thank you."

They started off again, Starling matching his pace to hers. She could tell he didn't like it. He was like a spirited racehorse being held back when it wants to run all out, pulling at the bit until it gets its' way. But he remained with her, which she was quite thankful for.

He led her expertly through the streets ignoring all the hawkers calling out their wares. She was entranced by everything. She wished that Starling would go slower so she could look over the vendors' wares, but he never glanced at anything. Finally they reached the end of the market and Starling stopped when they reached the town boundary. All that was before them was vast pasture lands where cow-like creatures grazed.

He turned to her with a veiled expression and asked, "Can you ride?"

"Ride? A horse?

"Yes."

"A little, I never really had an opportunity to try."

"Then here's the best time." he walked over to the shadow of one of the last buildings and ducked into an opening. In a moment he returned leading two horses; one silvery white, the other a deep golden color. He looped the reins over a fence post and waited for Cinderella to come closer.

"Which one?" she asked.

"Either."

She especially liked the way the white one looked so she walked slowly up to it. She held her hand tentatively out and it sniffed her. Not finding anything to eat it snorted and raised it head and looked out over the fields.

"Come on." Starling said as he boosted her swiftly into the saddle.

She clung tightly on and he leapt onto the back of the golden horse after untying the reins. He kept hold of the lead to her horse while he kicked his horse forward and led the way into the pastures. Cinderella's horse followed and after awhile she felt quite comfortable with the gentle swaying motion of the animal. It was a good horse and followed Starling's quietly.

After awhile she called to him, "Where are we going?"

"Somewhere."

"But where?"

"Is it your business?" he snapped turning around in the saddle. His face was angry and Cinderella wished she hadn't asked. He instantly regretted turning on her like that, but he wasn't one to apologize. They rode on in silence.

After awhile longer they reached the edge of the pasture land and Cinderella found themselves on the edge of a plateau. Starling dismounted and helped her down. She walked stiffly forward to see the view, but she before she had gone two steps she found herself yanked backwards into Starling's arms. She struggled and he turned her around.

"Don't walk. You're liable to fall over the edge. Come this way." he took her hand and led her to the side, up a step-like rocky portion of ground that the horses couldn't have climbed.

When they reached the top, Starling took Cinderella over to the cliff side and pointed out where they had just been. Cinderella saw the horses, and directly in-front of them, where she had been headed, was a vertical precipice that ended in the sea at a dizzyingly long drop. The shrubbery concealed the amount of ground available to walk on and she would have unknowingly walked over the edge if it hadn't been for Starling. She glanced at him to let him know she was thankful for his interference, but he was gazing out at the sea with a strange look in his dark brown eyes. He felt her gaze and looked back down at her. The look was still in his eyes and she felt strangely disconcerted by it.

She shifted her gaze back to the view of the land and said quietly, "It's very beautiful."

"Mm-hmm."

"Why did we come up here?"

"For something." he shifted away from her and walked into some of the overgrowth. Cinderella paused a moment, and then plunged in after him. She could hardly see anything and suddenly she bumped into something very solid.

"Slow down, and go a bit quieter will you." Starling's voice said in-front of her. She realized it was him that she had just run into.

"I'm sorry." she murmured. She stepped beside him, and he clasped her hand in his and led her the rest of the way through the brush.

They came out into a small clearing. He let go her hand and crossed the clearing in two long strides. He kneeled down and put his hand into a thorny bush. His face remained unemotional – even as the thorns jabbed into his flesh. In a moment, he had pulled out a tin box. He took a silver chain out from inside his shirt. A small key hung off of it and he used it to unlock the box. Cinderella couldn't see what was inside, but he pulled something out of it and stuck it in his coat pocket. After locking the box he returned it to its hiding place. Then he stood and looked at Cinderella.

"Ready to go?" a slight twinkle glittered in his eyes. He suddenly reminded her of a mischievous imp.

Yes?" she answered unsurely.

He held out his hand and she took it timidly. He led her into the brush, but she could tell they weren't headed back to the horses.

"Where—" she began to question him.

"Hush." he cut her short.

She remained silent until they reached the edge of the wooded area. When they stepped out Cinderella found herself terrifyingly close to the edge of a steep precipice. Starling held tightly to her and led her deftly along the edge till they came to wider ground.

"Where are we?" she asked.

"Here." Starling replied smiling for once at her. She looked ahead and saw for the first time a strange hut. They walked up to it, Starling still holding onto her. They reached the hut and Starling led her inside after unlocking the door with a key that he took out of his pocket.

The late afternoon light sifted through the leafy roof and Cinderella gasped at the vast collection of shells. The ones in the cabin aboard the ship was nothing compared to here. A breeze knocked tiny shells strung together against each other creating a soft, tinkling sound. Cinderella gazed mutely in astonishment. Sunlight glistened on some of the shells making them appear like jewels. Gold veining wove through the shell closest to Cinderella and she couldn't get over the amazing colors marbled in each one. There were shells so large she could have worn it like a hat, others that were smaller than her fingernail.

"These are all yours?" she breathed as she stared at everything trying to see each shell.

"Yes. I only keep a few on ship. I brought some with me to leave here." Starling answered as he pulled a few shells from his capacious coat pocket and found spots for them amongst his other ones.

"Do you live here? When you're not at sea I mean."

"Not exactly. We come often to this port. If we dock long enough I may stay up here for a few days, to be alone. Father said this island is where I was born and where he used to live when he was young, before becoming a pirate. I did a lot of things here when I was growing up. Father built this hut and we would live here when he wasn't taking me sailing. It holds a lot of memories for me."

"Does your mother live here then?" she asked naively thinking that a woman would not possibly wish to remain aboard a pirate ship.

Starling's face hardened and he said, "That isn't any business of yours is it?"

"I'm-I'm sorry." she turned away from him and walked over to the opposite side of the hut to see the shells there better.

"Cinderella. I-I didn't mean to snap at you. The fact is I never knew my mother. Father won't speak of her…"

Cinderella turned back to face him. He was standing in the doorway, the light shining through framed his impressive figure. His eyes looked beseechingly at her and she smiled at him. Not another word was spoken on the matter.

Starling showed her his favorite shells. Which she agreed were the finest parts of his collection.

"Do you mind me asking why you collect them? I mean why you started to?" she asked.

Starling was quiet for so long that she thought he would never respond. Finally he said, "When I was very young, Father would always take me to the beach and we would find shells together. When I was old enough to be left alone, he would go on sailing trips without me, but he would always bring me back a shell from whatever islands they stopped at. He told me that the shells were magical and would let me hear whatever was going on wherever he was in the sea. I now just find them something interesting to look at. I don't like going to the pubs and drinking my nights away with wenches like all of the other pirates. I suppose you could say that I am the only pirate that doesn't truly behave like an ordinary pirate."

"Any why the difference? Did you only get pulled into piracy because of your father?" Starling was opening up a whole new side of him that she would never have guessed.

He shrugged, "Father would never have made me be a pirate if I didn't wish. I could have stayed here on this island or gone to any island I wanted if I had asked him. I don't mind the life of a pirate, I just choose not to behave like a typical one. We are gentlemen pirates after all, I would think you could have told that from my father."

"He does seem very nice." Cinderella murmured.

"He insisted that I learn everything that a nobleman would while growing up. He taught me everything I know. His book collection is his pride. Giving you access to them was a huge privilege." he stopped talking and looked outside, the sun was beginning to dip low into the sky. "We should go ahead and get back before it gets dark or else we'll be stranded up here for the night. It's too dangerous a path to travel without light."

He led her from the hut, back into the undergrowth, and to the waiting horses. It was shorter getting back than it had been coming there. He lifted her gently into the saddle then leading her horse once more they rode back to the town. Starling took her to the ship where they would stay for the night instead of in town at an inn like many of the crew were doing.

They stayed in port another two days. Captain Albatross employed a new cook; an older man with sun wrinkled skin, bald, kindly green eyes, and a laugh that could carry a mile. He was nice to all, a good cook, and was very excited to have Cinderella helping him and teaching him some new recipes.

Cinderella liked him immediately and she enjoyed helping him. No one could complain about the food, which was better than any other ship's in the world. Every day, Cinderella would get up, help make breakfast for the crew, go up to the deck and watch the sailors, possibly swab decks, or anything other small chores that Starling might find for her to do. But normally, he had nothing for her, so she would watch the sea being sliced through by the ship, read books from the captain's cabin, or talk to Starling who seemed far more open to her and was nearby almost constantly.

She would then help the cook with the luncheon, and finally supper. She would watch the sunset afterwards and it was this time of day that was her favorite. Starling would always join her near the bowsprit and they would watch the sunset together, sometimes in silence, other times chatting about anything that came to mind. She told him about her family, the bakery, the work in the palace, the queen's grudge against her, the horrible Hodgesheds, the ball, meeting the prince and becoming engaged to him. And he always listened attentively, asking her questions and truly interested in everything she had to tell him.

He in turn would tell her about growing up on the island and then moving onto the ship. He explained everything about how the ship worked – though she surprised him by how much William had already taught her. He told her the tales of the many battles he had been in, the story behind his scar, interesting facts about the crew members – which were the only family he knew.

She was pleasantly surprised by how intelligent he was and they had many pleasant debates. He would pick out some of the books from his father's collection and have her read them and then discuss the topics. Most of the books covered politics and economics, science and philosophy. She didn't think she would actually enjoy reading the books when he first asked he too, but she found it all quite interesting especially since someone of her lowly birth would never have been able to learn such things. He loved her different points of view. Growing up in the kingdom she had been taught to see things from a far different perspective than his life as a pirate had.

They both enjoyed and craved each other's company. It wasn't long before they had become fast friends. She could confide anything to him and knew that he would not judge or make fun of her. And he had turned out to be a completely different person than when they had first met.

Cinderella began to actually not feel so sad that she hadn't been able to marry Royal. In her talks with Sterling she often found herself comparing the two men. From the few talks with Royal she had gotten the impression that he was very much self-centered and didn't care all that much about her personally. Sterling though would listen to her chatter for hours and remember everything she told him. She was very glad that she had found such a friend.

Chapter 16

The ship cut through the water like a knife through butter. Royal leaned over the side watching the waves part for them. Eric lounged beside him, not very happy to be out to sea, but knowing that it would be one of the last trips that he would have to take with Prince Royal. Once the prince married Ella, Royal wouldn't be leaving nearly as often. Unless Ella loved the sea. He was just hoping that he wouldn't have to come anymore for surely they would want the fewest amount of people about as possible. Maybe he would be able to stay at the palace or the prince would reward him for his loyal service by making him a lord. Either way there was always plenty to keep his attention at the palace, such as getting to know that pretty handmaiden a bit better. Eric was startled out of his thoughts by Royal standing straight and calling out,

"Isla Prehendere! There it is!"

Eric turned and saw for himself the small, dark mass of land taking shape on the horizon. Neither him nor the prince had ever been to the isle of banishment, so he didn't know what to expect. They had been blessed with good weather all the way, and since their ship was quicker than the prisoner ship, they had made it there in half the time. In the next day they would be able to weigh anchor and set foot the isle. They would find Ella and give her the happy news that she was innocent and had received a royal pardon and the utmost apology from the king and queen. They had absolutely no clue that she had never even seen the island.

They made it to the isle in the morning and found the prisoner ship in the bay.

"I thought they would have left by now." Prince Royal mused to himself. Normally the ship would bring the prisoners, dispose of them, maybe stay for a little while longer if the weather were bad and then go back to Bleu Evine. It had been two months and the ship was still here! Royal was very curious now.

They were greeted with the greatest honor befitting the prince. The steward of the isle gave them all the best food and treatment that was manageable for them.

"What brings His Royal Highness to this lowly isle?" the steward asked bowing so low that his neatly trimmed goatee nearly brushed the floor.

"I have come for a prisoner. She was wrongfully sent here and I want to take her back. She's innocent. I have the proper papers for you as well." and he brought out the rolled parchment containing the king's royal seal.

"What is her name, my Lord?"

"Ella. I mean Cinderella."

"Cinderella?" the steward scratched his chin while he thought.

"Yes."

"I have never heard that name before, my Prince. I keep a very thorough record and I would remember such an unusual name."

"She would have just arrived, all by herself. The ship in the bay brought her here."

"No, my Lord. There were no prisoners aboard that ship."

"What?!" Royal rose from his chair wondering what sort of lies the steward was trying to tell him.

"You can speak to the captain if you would like."

"That I do!"

The steward trotted off to find Captain Vincent. While he was gone William, the sailor, came walking through the hall near the room that Prince Royal and Eric were waiting in.

"Not here! How could she not be here! That ship had to bring her! Where else could she be?!" Royal was pacing and gesturing animatedly.

"I don't know, Royal."

"Royal?" William thought. *"Prince Royal? Then he must be looking for Cinders."* William unthinkingly pushed the door open and walked inside.

Royal and Eric stopped talking and they looked at William wonderingly.

"Are you the captain?" Roy asked skeptically.

"N-no, Your Highness. I am only a sailor on the prison ship."

"What are you doing in here then?!"

"I beg your pardon. I was walking by and I heard you talking. You're looking for Cinders aren't you?"

"Cinders?"

"Yes, I mean, Cinderella."

"Yes! Where is she?!" Royal cried out.

"She isn't here. She never made it here…"

"Where is she then?!" Roy stepped towards the young man, gripping him roughly by his shirt collar

"We were attacked by pirates. She was taken captive."

The news stunned both the prince and Eric into complete silence. How does one respond to the news that the person that you are in love with is now a captive of pirates? There was always the possibility she wasn't even alive even more.

"Pirates?" Roy asked, letting go of the sailor and stumbling back to his seat.

"Yes, my Lord. I was there. I saw it all. We were going to come back to Bleu Evine after it happened, but there was a bad storm and we ended up stranded on this accursed place."

"What's your name?"

"William."

"Well, William, you knew Ella?"

"Yes, I knew Cinders quite well."

"Good. Then will you come with me, we will search the seas until I find her!"

"Gladly, my Prince! I have been asking Captain Vincent to search for her. But he wouldn't. Well, said that he couldn't since he is the captain of a royal ship and would have to have the permission of the king to do so. No one will help me go search for her!"

"You're a good man, William. Get ready, We leave in the morning. Meet us at the bay before the tide goes out. I trust that you will be able to remember what ship it was that took her, won't you?"

"Of course. I've seen her before now."

"Good. Till then, William."

Will bowed and left, quite happy that he was able to go help save Cinderella from those murderous, vile pirates.

Chapter 14

"Cella!"

Cinderella turned at the sound of Starling's voice. It had an odd inflection in it that she had never heard and she wondered as to what it could mean. He had taken to calling her "Cella" since he said that Cinderella was just too long to say all the time and he preferred short names. So she chose to call him Star in return. He had objected at first but he soon grew to like hearing her sweet voice calling him.

"What is it?" she asked.

"There's a ship nearby, we're going to take it. I want you to stay in the cabin until it's all over."

Cella then realized what he was trying to say. The pirates were going to attack a merchant vessel that they had spotted.

"Must you?" she asked.

"Cella, that's what we do. We're pirates. How do we make a living otherwise?"

"Star—"

"No debating with me now! It's what we do, and we are going to do it. But don't worry, Cap'n is a fine gentleman and he doesn't shed blood unless it be absolutely necessary."

Cinderella wasn't entirely convinced, but she obeyed Starling and stayed in her cabin.

A few of the braver sailors aboard the merchant ship tried to put up a futile fight against the pirates, but they were quickly subdued without loss of any life. Captain Albatross was a true gentleman pirate and only took what supplies would either bring great profit or what was needed for his own crew. Then he departed with an extravagant bow and, "Thankee kindly." The pirate ship was turned away and very soon there was no sign of the merchants.

"Cella, you can come out now." Starling called to her as he knocked on the door.

Cinderella came out and looked at Starling with a disapproving stare.

"No one was harmed. The merchants are fine, and we have increased our stores." Star informed her.

"But you stole." Cinderella accused.

"That's a pirate's life, Cella. I already told you."

"That doesn't make it right."

"Maybe so, but at least we aren't ruthless, bloody pirates that sail the seas just to kill and plunder."

"Why can't you just become a respectable sailor?"

"That isn't able to be done now. I'm a pirate – forever."

"You can change! You're not like *them*."

"No, Cella. Once a pirate, always a pirate. I'm unmistakably a pirate and I would be hung as one. No one wants a pirate on their ship and I would die if I were not to go to sea."

Cella sighed and walked away from him. He looked downcast but he let her be. They didn't even watch the sunset together as they normally would. They had broached this topic in their debates before and it always came back to the same thing. She would never approve and he could never hope to sway her to his point of view.

The next day, Captain Albatross proclaimed a "holiday" because of their good fortune from the merchant vessel. The cook prepared a delicious feast, the rum ran freely, and everyone was in high spirits; everyone except for Starling and Cinderella. She was not happy because of the reason why they were celebrating and Starling wasn't happy because Cella wasn't. The musicians played lively tunes throughout the day, and the crew who were besotted with rum would jump to their wobbly legs and try to dance, most would trip over their own feet and fall to the deck laughing with their mates. The captain sat nearby watching and laughing with his crew. He hadn't touched any of the cheap rum and neither had Starling. Cinderella absolutely refused any sort of the "vile drink" as she called it. So the three sat by watching the merry-making and eating some of the food that the cook had expertly prepared.

Captain Albatross hated the fact that Starling and Cinderella, who he looked upon as a daughter, should be so unhappy looking. When a lull came in the music, the captain went over and talked to the head musician. When they started their songs up again, it was an entirely new tune.

"Now you two, I want ye to teach this group of unreformed men the finer art o' dancin'." Captain Albatross said addressing the only two silent people on the ship.

"No offense, Cap'n but I don't feel like dancing." Starling muttered. Cinderella added that she really didn't feel like it either.

The crew, though, insisted, along with the captain, and soon they found themselves somehow on their feet with Cinderella in Starling's arms.

"I suppose we have no choice in the matter." he grunted sullenly.

They started to dance to the song that the musicians were playing and the crew cheered them on. Cinderella was shocked to find that Starling knew how to dance as perfectly as any gentleman back home. He never missed a step and led her confidently through the entire dance. When it was over he bowed deeply and would have gone back to sitting by the side, except that the musicians started yet another song and the crew insisted that they dance one more. Cinderella, after that first dance, actually felt fine with dancing again and so Starling conceded. But as they moved through the steps, Cinderella started to falter and her face paled. Starling noticed and abruptly stopped.

"Is something wrong?" he practically whispered.

Total silence reigned aboard the ship. Everyone, even in their drunken states, could see the change in Cella. She shook her head and answered hoarsely, "I'm sorry, Star, I want to go to my cabin now." he let go of her and she walked swiftly across deck and closed the door behind her.

There was a confused silence by her departure, then the musicians started up a rousing ditty and soon all was forgotten except by the captain and Starling.

"Do ye want me to go see her or you?" the captain asked after the crew resumed their gaiety and Starling was sitting alongside the captain.

"I shall. In a moment." Starling answered.

Only when he was sure that she had time to compose herself and get over whatever had ailed her did he get up and go to his cabin. He knocked softly and when there was no answer asked, "Cella? Can I talk you?"

There was dead silence, and right when Starling was nearly ready to leave, the door opened and Cella looked out.

"What is it, Star?"

"Can I come in?"

Cinderella hesitated, then opened the door wider. Starling walked in and sat down in one of the chairs. Cinderella shut the door and walked over, taking the other chair. He studied her for a moment then asked, "What happened out there?"

"Nothing really."

"Cella. I thought I was your friend. You can trust me. You've been telling me everything up till now."

"I… It-it was just the song that they were playing… It reminded me of another time that I… It was just some sad memories."

"You're home?"

"Yes… I danced with Prince Royal to that song. It was the very first time that we danced… D-do you understand?"

Starling sat silent, staring at her. One topic she would hardly ever speak of was the prince and their engagement. He wanted to know more and had plenty of questions but was loath to pry. Eventually he nodded and said, "Of course I do, Cella. It's all right. I'll just tell anyone that asks that you just didn't feel very well and wanted to retire to your cabin. Is there anything that you want? A drink or food?"

"No, thank you, Star. I'm fine. Really."

Starling accepted her answer and got up to leave.

"Star?"

"Yes."

"We are friends. Just so you know." she said with a smile.

He smiled back and left the cabin.

"Well?" Captain Albatross asked as Starling took a seat beside him again to watch the crew in their partying.

"She just doesn't feel very well at the moment. I'm sure she'll be all right presently."

"She did seem odd all day. I suppose it does take time to get used to a pirate's life."

"Indeed." Starling replied, but he wondered how much that really had to do with everything.

Chapter 16

"We've been out here a month! Still there is no sighting or sign that the ship was ever here! No one has seen the pirates!" Royal was beside himself. He was upset at the time it was taking to find Cinderella and upset that there was nothing he could do to get it done any quicker.

"This area relies on the pirates most of the time." William spoke up, "Most will harbor pirates and even lie to you, Prince Royal, to protect them and their access to the money that the pirates will bring in to them."

"If I find anyone lying to me! So help me, I'll punish them severely!"

"Your Highness, don't worry, we will find them eventually. We're coming up to a port that is very popular with pirates. We're sure to hear something of the ship we seek there."

"You're certain?"

"Entirely."

Royal accepted William's advise and was quiet till they got to port. There they heard the news that yes, Captain Albatross' ship had been there not two weeks ago. They had headed south but were bound to be back sometime, hopefully, soon. William advised the prince to wait at the island, he was sure that the pirates would turn up shortly. So wait they did.

"Star, are we headed anywhere in particular?' Cella and Star were leaning against the ship railing watching the sparkling blue water ripple beneath them. Dolphins were chirping alongside, jumping out of the water and doing intricate flips trying to catch the attention of the crew.

"We sail the seas, find ships, and return to port only when our provisions are low or we need to make repairs."

"Is there no purpose in all of your lives then?"

"There is point… Until you learn our ways, Cella, you'll never understand."

"I'm sorry, Star. I always seem to be fussing at you about this."

Starling smiled warmly at her. It had been a week since the raid on the merchant ship and Cella was acting like herself again. Starling had noticed that she seemed a lot happier than normal.

"Cella?"

"Yes?'

"Are you happy here?"

Cinderella couldn't answer at first. She wasn't sure how to. She thought a moment and then slowly said, "I'm happy to an extent. I would be happier if I were with my parents. I do miss them very much; and the bakery, I miss the work there. I miss the land. Not that I don't like the sea, it's just not what I am used to…"

"I understand that entirely. I grew up mostly on the sea and I miss it terribly if I'm on shore too long. But what about the prince?" Starling knew he was taking a risk in asking, but he had to know.

"Well, I-I don't know really. I thought I did… He was really quite nice. I suppose that yes I miss him and…"

"It's all right, Cella. I understand." he butted in softly.

She looked up at him with her eyes expressing her thanks. He always seemed to know how she felt and he was so kind and respectful of everything. He never pressed her if she didn't want to answer. He was a true gentleman and nothing like the other pirates or even the captain.

"Cella, I have something for you."

She looked surprised then a smile glimmered on her face. He loved to see her smile, she was so pretty when she did. His breath caught in his throat and he smiled back. His heart was hammering so hard he thought that she would be able to hear it.

"Come on, I want to give it to you now." he led her back to her cabin. He shut the door behind them and she sat on the edge of the cot. He walked over to his sea trunk. She had never opened it but knew it was his personal belongings. Besides she couldn't have unlocked it anyway. He produced a key from his pocket and unlocked the heavy padlock on the trunk. Several shirts lay on top. He shoved these aside and, at the bottom, he took out, very gently, a velvet pouch. This he handed to her.

Cinderella opened the pouch in curiosity and was surprised to see two very delicate, crystal slippers. She gently took them out of the pouch and looked them over. The light from the window glittered on them and they seemed to be made of a rainbow. Swirls were etched along the side, the heel was short, and they looked entirely too fragile to wear.

"Try them on." Starling urged.

She looked doubtfully at them, but removed her threadbare shoes and slipped the elegant ones on. They fit her perfectly. Starling helped her stand. The slippers bore her weight, and they were the most comfortable shoes that she had ever worn.

"These are so beautiful! I've never seen their like anywhere! How on earth can I wear them? They seem far too fragile!"

"I heard they were magical."

"I could believe that."

"Supposedly the slippers fit themselves to the first person to wear them, then only that person can ever wear them. I did hear that they can't be broken, at least not by being worn."

"Why are you giving these to me?"

"You're the first girl that I have—" he wanted to say loved, but instead shrugged and said, "have ever wanted to give them to."

Cinderella gazed into his dark eyes and said, "Thank you, Starling. Thank you very much! It is a gift fit for a queen!"

He gazed back at her with a look in his eyes that she had never noticed before, one that could only be attributed to a person in love. Impulsively he leaned down quite close to her beautiful face and she automatically leaned up towards him. He slipped his arms around her, pulling her a bit closer till their lips were almost touching. Right then, a knock sounded at the door and Captain Albatross' voice called out, "Starling, boy? Are ye there?"

The spell between the two was instantly broken, and they bashfully stepped away from each other. Starling strode to the door, threw it open, and answered his father's call for him.

"Ah, Starling. What are ye doin'?"

"I wanted to give Cella a gift." he huffed in impatience.

Captain Albatross looked over at her. He didn't say anything about her bright red face, but instead asked, "What was this gift?"

She walked over to him, the shoes making a clinking like tiny silver bells, and showed the slippers to the captain.

"I forgot that you had those, boy! A very handsome gift indeed! Starling," He returned his attention back to why he had come. "I'm takin' us back to Fleur Shea."

"So soon?"

"Aye. I think it will be best to go back there. Get rid of the extra loot that we don't need to be carryin' 'round with us."

"Very well then, Captain."

"If you'll come and help me?"

"Of course." Starling turned back to Cinderella. "Goodnight, Cella." a vague hint of the previous feeling that he had showed still glimmered in his eyes.

She smiled cordially trying to calm her racing heart and replied, "Good-night. And thank you again."

Starling and the captain bowed and left the cabin. Once they were gone she sat down on the bed and pulled the shoes off. She turned them around in her hands, tracing the details and marveling at the gift. She wondered where on earth he could have got them. But her thoughts quickly drifted to Starling. She couldn't get the look of his eyes out of her mind the intense stare and the way it had felt to be held in his arms so close to him. He clearly was in love with her, but what were her feelings for him?

She fell into a confused sleep. She dreamed that she was getting ready to be married to Prince Royal but before the ceremony could commence an enraged Starling appeared and carried her off to the pirate ship. She woke with racing heart and realized that she actually liked the outcome of her dream. Could it be she was falling for a pirate?

Chapter 16

"Royal! ROYAL!" Eric burst into the room that the prince was staying in. His wavy hair hung all over his forehead from running, his eyes were wide and excited, and he was breathless both from the run and the news he carried.

"Eric, what is it?"

"The Pirates! We-we saw-saw the ship. Will claims— He says it is the one!"

Royal was immediate action. "We'll go out and meet them before they make port!" he led the way back to the docks and roused the crew and soldiers. As soon as the tide was right, they were out of port and headed towards the ship that was sailing towards them.

☙

"What ship is that?" Cinderella asked Starling. They were leaning out over the gunwales watching the shore get closer, and now they had spotted a ship leaving port, headed towards them.

Starling squinted his eyes from the sunlight and stared at the ship. He suddenly gave a shocked gasp and scrambled across deck to where the captain was.

"Cap'n!" he yelled.

"Starling?"

"The ship, Sir!"

"I see it."

"But did you see the flag?"

"I can't make it out. I sent the boy for me telescope."

"No need. It's a king's ship."

"Ye sure?"

"Aye."

"Avast me mates! Turn about!" Captain Albatross was not going to meet a king's ship under any circumstances.

The sailors hopped immediately to their captain's orders and the ship was turned around.

"What's wrong, Starling?" Cinderella asked.

"It's a king's ship."

"What's wrong about that?"

"There's bound to be soldiers. If we are caught, it's the hangman's noose for all of us."

"Oh—" a strange look came into her eyes and she asked suddenly, "Could it be Roy?!"

"The prince?" a bitter sound crept into Starling's voice and Cella bit her lip to prevent saying anything else. "Cella, I— you're supposed to be on Isla Prehendere."

"But he… Never mind, it's impossible."

"Of course." but Starling didn't sound to sure and he encouraged all the crew to do their best to put as much distance between the ship and theirs.

※

"What's going on?" Eric asked.

"They must have spotted us, they're turning away." William answered.

Prince Royal stood beside them. He was alert and seemingly calm, but William noticed the way he gripped the railing of the ship and his tanned skin showed pale white.

"We're the faster ship. We *will* catch them." Will assured them all. And William was correct. By the time they caught the pirate ship, the sun had set, but they stayed nearby all night. By the time the dawn broke, the ships were ready to do battle.

"I don't want to risk hurting Ella. Put up the truce flag." Royal commanded.

※

"The truce flag?" Starling was stunned. Never had a king's ship surrendered before a fight.

"It might be trick, we'll wait and see. But be on the alert."

They waited till the ships were close enough that the captain's could yell across to each other. Starling had forced Cella to remain in the cabin.

"We're wanting a prisoner that we believe is aboard your ship!" Prince Royal yelled across.

"What prisoner be ye talkin' 'bout?"

Starling knew and he clenched his fists angrily. He didn't want them to take her back! If only they could get rid of this ship and Cella need never know. He was sure he could convince her to forget the prince and marry him, and then they could be together forever. But plans didn't always go accordingly.

"The prisoner is a girl. Her name is Ella."

"We have no girl named Ella."

William leaned over and whispered to remind Royal, "She's Cinderella, Sire."

"It's Cinderella!" Royal yelled back.

Captain Albatross remained silent then asked cautiously, "Why ye be wantin' this particular girl?"

"She was supposed to be banished! I was told she was captured by you! She's been declared innocent and I want to return her to her home!"

"I'll see what we can do for ye, my Prince." he turned to Starling. "Well boy, she's innocent. That is the prince; her love."

"Maybe not anymore." Starling muttered.

109

"What was that, boy?'

"Nothing, Cap'n. What do you want me to do?"

"Go ask your Cella what she wants to do."

Starling swallowed hard and walked to the cabin. He knocked and Cinderella flung it open.

"Star?"

"Cella, I came to ask you… W-well see th-there's…"

"Star, what is it?" she smiled encouragingly.

"It's the— no I won't!" his eyes lit up suddenly as if on fire and Cinderella stepped back from him half afraid. He was talking to himself, "I won't! I swear I won't let them!"

"Starling?"

༄

"They're taking too long. Why negotiate with pirates? Attack them I say!" Royal suddenly exclaimed.

The ships were already rather close, and with a few careful maneuvers, they were soon close enough for a plank to be laid across for boarding the pirates vessel. This the soldiers did before the pirates knew what they were up to. The pirate ship was swarming with soldiers in a moment, and Prince Royal, flanked by the captain,and Eric walked up to Captain Albatross.

"I demand you to return, Ella!"

"I sent me bosun to find out for ye. This tain't an honorable thing ye be doin', me Prince."

"Honorable?" Royal snorted in disgust. "Such as you would not know the meaning."

Starling heard the commotion and tramping of the soldiers. He spun around, and when he saw all of the men, he flew into a serious rage. He slammed the door on Cella and went up to his father in a few steps.

"You have no right! We were negotiating!" he screeched at the prince.

Royal hardly glanced at the tall, young man. He remained focused on the captain, "Return Ella, and, possibly, I may spare some of your lives."

At the threat of death looming over them, Starling unsheathed his sword and in a moment would have killed the prince if it hadn't been for his father laying a hand on his arm.

"No, Starling me lad."

Starling glared in as much hatred as he could at Royal, then his gaze came to rest on a sailor behind them.

"You?!" he yelled recognizing William. "You led them to us!"

William turned pale. He didn't want to cross swords with this pirate again. He took a step back and stumbled. But he knocked into a pirate, who, so shaken up, thought that he was being attacked by the sailor. He drew his sword, and if it hadn't been for William entirely loosing his balance would have had another dead sailor to his record. William righted himself, and drew his own sword. Before any captain, prince, or boatswain could utter a sound, a full-scale battle was raging alongside them.

Starling took the opportunity and lashed out at the prince. But Eric was quicker and parried his blow to save his friend. Royal wasted no time in loosening his sword and joined the fray.

Cinderella heard the horrible noises and stayed inside her cabin terrified. After some time, the battle noises faded away until there was total silence. After some moments, the clop of shoes was heard outside the cabin door, it was thrown open and Cinderella screeched in fear. She regained herself when she saw,

"William!" she rushed gladly forward and fell into his arms. He hugged her and then held her at arms length to look her over.

"Are you hurt? Did they harm you?" he asked in concern.

"No! No, I'm fine! How-how? I'm so happy to see you Will!"

He smiled at her and even his grey eyes didn't seem quite as sad as normal.

"Come on, Prince Royal is here."

"Royal?" Cinderella could hardly believe her ears. But the thought of seeing him brought a sudden anxiety to her that she wasn't expecting. And she didn't feel as happy as she should have.

"Come on, Cinders. We'll take you home."

Cinderella followed him in a daze. The ship was a dreadful sight, and she wanted to get sick. Dead pirates and soldiers lay everywhere. Wounded moaned nearby or wandered around stupidly.

William tried to shield her from the sight and took her up to where Royal was standing, but then Cinderella cried out in anguish, "Starling!" just as Royal cried out joyfully, "Ella!" she pulled away from William and rushed over to the inert form of the bosun. She sank down beside him.

He was lying on his front, his face was turned to the side and was deathly white. Blood stained the deck beneath him and his sword lay shoved across the deck.

"Oh, Starling!" she sobbed. she touched him gently, tracing the pale scar across his face. She could see no sign of life in him.

"Cinders?" William's voice broke in on her grief. She turned her tear filled eyes up to her friend. He didn't say anything but helped her stand. Then she saw Royal. She looked at him as if she didn't recognize him.

He too stared, hardly recognizing the young woman. She was tanned a light brown and her brown hair had been bleached the sun to a dark blonde. "Ella? We came to take you home." he said as she walked past him.

She didn't say anything but instead followed them over to their ship, leaving the pirate ship with all its death behind.

Royal decided to just leave the pirates, why bother taking them in to hang when most were already dead, especially the most important ones being the captain and the boatswain.

Chapter 17

"He's alive me lads." the ship's doctor had been busy tending to everyone. He had come up to Starling and, ever so gently, he had his men take him to the cabin so he could patch up the first-mate.

Starling woke up about three hours later. He had been seriously wounded. A sword had punctured him right above the heart. He had lost consciousness, and everyone had given him up for dead. No one could believe that Starling, the best fighter that ever sailed the seas, had actually been wounded. It was said that he was wounded by the prince who, from the reports of everyone that had seen him fighting, was Starling's equal. They had been locked in a stale-mate for some time, until the prince's valet had come up and attacked Starling from the side – two against the one – with one being as good a match as possible for the bosun. It was an entirely unfair fight. But at least the prince didn't know the signs of life in someone so dead looking.

Weeks passed and Starling got stronger. Soon he was able to leave his cabin and walk about the ship. It was then that he was informed that Captain Albatross had been killed and Cinderella taken away by the prince. The remaining crew couldn't tell which news he took worse.

"Starling. I need to talk you." it was the doctor. He had been member of the crew ever since Starling had been born. He had been the closest to the captain besides Star, and he had Starling's utmost trust and respect.

"Yes, Doctor?"

"There's something that the Cap'n wanted me to tell you on the event of his death. I think you're able to hear it now. There was something that he kept secret from you. The fact is, you weren't his son."

"What?!"

"No, he took you when you were just a baby. He named you, called you his, and everyone treated you like that. To me only did he ever tell the entire truth. The rest o' the crew thought you were an orphan that he took pity on and brought with him. But I know the truth as to your parentage."

"And who did he say are my parents?"

"They be Leander and Octavia. King and Queen of Bleu Evine."

Starling was too stunned to speak.

"I have proof to back up the claim." The doctor added and produced a packet from his coat pocket. With trembling hands, Starling undid the leather ties. Inside was a baby's outfit made of the softest velvet and embroidered in gold thread. Surely only someone of high birth would wear such an outfit. The other items included with it were a folded piece of paper and a golden signet ring on a chain. The signet was bearing the seal of Bleu Evine. The paper looked to be like journal entry. It was written in tiny, dainty script, quite elegant and refined. At the bottom was the entry:

"Twins were born. Two boys. The younger is like me and much smaller than the other. We have named him Royal. The eldest is more like Leander. We have chosen his name to be Sterling. We are so very happy! But Leander is eager to leave this place. He says that Fleur Shea is not a safe place to stay for long. I'm sure he is

right. It is a supposed pirate haunt. I would be terrified to meet a pirate. If only we were home at the palace. I hear Leander coming back now. No, that isn't Leander's step—"

It ended abruptly and Starling was stunned. "I am the older twin?" he asked hoarsely.

"Aye."

"Why?"

"You were to be a ransom. But Captain Albatross liked you so well, he couldn't part with you. He took these things to prove your identity. Now he would want you to go back and claim your place."

"I can't."

"Why?"

"If this it true. That was my brother. I nearly killed him! I would have! He nearly killed me! I would be hung as a pirate and no one would believe my tale! I must remain a pirate now. It's my life."

"No! It's not! Cap'n never wanted you to have this life. That's why he wanted you to learn. That's why he treated you the way he did! He wanted to send you back, but he didn't want to lose you. After all those years you were truly a son to him. He told me where he kept those items hidden and he made me swear that if he died before he told you that I would tell you. Starling – Prince Sterling, it's time you went home."

Chapter 18

Cinderella was silent for over half of the trip. She was still dazed that she was being taken back to Bleu Evine. She had been told how the fake theft had happened and that she was now innocent. She couldn't explain why, but she didn't want to be with Royal. She knew that he had to have had a hand in Starling's death and she couldn't face him right then. Only to William could she almost be herself. She talked with him once she came out of her seclusion and renewed the friendship that they had shared.

"Cinders, you look particularly unhappy tonight. What's wrong?" William had joined Cinderella at the bow where she was leaning, watching the sunset.

Her shoulders were slumped, her comely face was clouded in grief, and her eyes were blurred with tears.

"Will, I am thankful to be going home and back to my parents – I missed them frightfully – but, as crazy as it sounds, I miss the pirates."

"How?!"

"They were good men! The captain was a true gentleman. And Starling…" she couldn't go on. The tears spilled over and she leaned down into her arms sobbing.

William comforted her and asked very softly, "Did you love him?"

After some time, once her tears had dried, Cinders raised herself back up to her full height. "Will, when I was at home and was going to marry Royal, I wanted to! I thought I loved him… Now, after being separated from him for so long, well I've realized that it was only an infatuation – a fantasy that I would marry the prince and become princess – that would appeal to any poor girl such as myself. I don't know him well enough to know if I could love him, but I know I didn't truly then and I don't now. I'm sure I could have learned to over time if we would have been married. When I was with you, I didn't want to think of it. I was too shocked over my banishment to even consider my true feelings for him. When I was taken by the pirates, and once I found out that I would not be treated ill or need fear them, I started to think about things like that. I wanted to go home – to be proven innocent – but I was still safe with them, and they had become my friends."

She stopped and Will encouraged her to go on.

"Well. One day, they were all dancing and then the captain had them play a waltz. Starling knew how to dance as fine as any gentleman at home and we danced together. Then the crew persuaded us to go again, but the song that they played was the one that Royal and I had danced to the very first time at the ball. I couldn't finish the dance and went to my cabin. Since I thought I would be with the pirates forever I hadn't thought much of what it might have been had I been home. But I couldn't stop thinking then. I had to explain to Star why I had left – he understood me. He always did… After I had cried and talked to myself about the whole matter I felt much better. As the days passed I began to realize that I was more homesick than lovesick. And I know for sure that I do not love Royal, not truly.

Yes, I loved Starling. He was so good and kind. He understood everything even when I didn't say it. He was—" she stopped and started crying again. William held her until her tears were once again dry.

"Cinders, it's all right. Things will work out for you. You don't have to marry Royal you know. Just tell him, explain to him. I'm sure he'll understand if he does care for you as much as he acts."

"After all he's done to get me back? He'll be so hurt."

"He'll learn to get over it." William stated a little harshly.

Cinderella turned her eyes back out to sea and looked into the distance. "I forgot them." she murmured sadly.

"Forgot what?"

"My shoes."

"You have shoes on."

"Starling gave me crystal slippers. They were magical he said. I left them in the cabin when you got me."

"I'm afraid they're lost to us now… I'm sorry, Cinders."

"It's all right. I just wish I had them to have something to remember him by."

☙

Royal was hurt that Ella didn't want to be with him. After all, he had worked so hard to prove her innocent and then he had been sailing everywhere for so long to rescue her. Did she love that obnoxious pirate? Had she fallen for that sailor William? He couldn't understand. Eric tried to console his master as to what he thought was the truth.

Cinderella was probably still in shock to be going home, the horrors of the battle on the ship probably scared most of her wits away and she was still recovering from that. It was also possible that some of the pirates had been her friends and seeing them dead was not comforting, William was a commoner like her and was easier to talk to as opposed to the prince. Besides Will had found her first on the ship after the battle. Eric had many explanations and most were near the truth, only he didn't reckon on Starling being the main cause for her sadness.

☙

Bleu Evine was eventually spotted, and Royal was finally able to talk to Ella.

"Ella, aren't you happy to be going home?"

"Of course! I missed my parents and the bakery very much!"

"What about me?" he asked with a sad expression on his handsome face.

"I missed you…"

Royal knew she wasn't telling him everything. He didn't know if he should press her into telling him the truth, but he thought better of it and decided to let her be.

"My mother is very sorry for what she did to you." he said changing the subject.

"I'm sure…"

"You don't sound as if you believe me."

"If I see her truly remorseful then I will believe it."

"You shall. We'll go directly there."

"But— as you wish…" she had wanted to tell him that she wished to go home to her dear parents and the familiar bakery, but to argue with Royal now would not have been polite. So she held her tongue, though she knew that Starling would have taken her straight there had he been the one bringing her home.

☙

"Royal! We were so worried about you! You were gone far too long ! And Cinderella, you have returned. I must express my deepest sympathy to you for banishing you that way. Please forgive me, child, and accept this home as yours now as well. We shall prepare the wedding of course and you and Royal can be very happy, presently." King Leander embraced them both.

Cinderella thanked him and assured him that she had forgiven any wrongs against her. She waited for the queen to say something. As she was waiting, she studied the king and queen. Royal was very much like his mother she noted. She knew that King Leander reminded her of someone, but she could not figure out whom. He was tall, strong, and quite handsome still for his age.

Queen Octavia walked gracefully forward and extended her hand to Cinderella. "My dear, I must apologize to you. It was my doing to have you so wrongfully blamed, and I shall live to forever regret it. The necklace that I had given to you, I want you to always remember me by it and the fact that I am truly happy that you shall be my son's wife."

"Thank you." Cinderella curtsied, truly the queen did seem remorseful. Gone was all the cold hostility that she had always regarded Cinderella with, and her smile was genuine.

"We shall have the wedding preparations started at once so that no more time is to be wasted!" Royal declared.

Now was the time that Cinderella had to say something. She opened her mouth, and taking a deep breath said, "I'm sorry. Royal, I can't marry you. Not right now. I'm not ready. Before I was. Or I thought I was. But now… I-I can't. Maybe later… Please try to understand."

Royal looked so hurt that Ella wished she could take it back – even if it meant her own unhappiness. After all, Starling was dead, who else was there to love now? She probably could learn to love Royal – over time – once she had forgotten Starling. Though she knew that could never happen.

"I see." Royal stated slowly. "Is… Does it have anything to do with William?" he asked.

"Who's William?" the king and queen asked.

Cinderella looked as surprised as them and asked, "William? You think I love him?"

"I do not know! Do you?"

"William is a dear friend! He was so kind to me and helped make the trip much more bearable! But I do not love him and he could never prevent me from marrying you if that is what I truly wanted to do."

Royal seemed relieved, but then a hard look came to his eyes and he asked so quietly that only Ella could hear, "It was that pirate." a muscle jerked in his cheek as Ella looked away in silence. By not speaking she told him as plainly as words that, yes, he was the sole reason.

"In time…" Royal mused. "Come I will take you to your parents now. We will postpone the wedding."

Cinderella thanked him with her eyes, but he didn't return her gaze. He led her stiffly to a waiting carriage and rode with her in silence to the little bakery. Her parents were overjoyed at the return of their dear daughter. Of course they had heard tales of her crime but never believed a word.

That night she told them her entire tale, from start to finish. She even told them about Starling and how much she loved him and now how she could not marry Royal because of him. They agreed that it was wisest to wait. After all, why marry a man and make both of them unhappy when she did not love him enough.

Chapter 19

Starling, Prince Sterling, did as the doctor had said. They turned the ship to Bleu Evine where he would try to make good his claim of being the prince.

They reached the port a little over a month after the return of Prince Royal and Ella.

Cinderella had since been living happily, for the most part, with her parents and working with them as she had always done, she had given up her place as maid at the palace. The prince called on her frequently and they would go for a ride and he would talk. She still refused him, wishing to wait. Slowly, the pain over Starling's death was going away. She missed him sorely and loved him desperately still, but she had started to notice how Royal was very much like him, in a finer, more cultured way. He wasn't as considerate or kind as Starling, nor did her understand her as well, but still his manner and bearing reminded her of her dead love. She didn't mind his presence, and she knew that before much longer she was sure to accept his proposal.

She knew she would never be as happy as she could have been had it been Starling instead of Royal, but the prince did seem to care very much for her. She tried to reason with herself that accepting Royal wouldn't be just to try to fill the emptiness in her heart. She tried to make herself believe that she could truly love him for himself.

Starling left the ship out to sea and took only a rowboat to the docks. He didn't want his remaining crew to be captured. He had told them all of who he was, and they all encouraged him to go claim his place as the prince.

He drew considerable attention to himself as he walked through the streets. He had a mind to stop and look for Cella's bakery and see if she was there. But he was sure that she had married Royal, his brother, after their return. It was too long now for him to hope that she was not princess. After all, he couldn't blame her, she thought he was dead. Besides, he had never known for sure if she reciprocated his love. For all he knew she had truly loved Royal and only cared for him as a close friend.

He reached the palace gates, forced admittance to the grounds, and walked up to the large doors. Here the guards firmly refused to allow such an uncouth villain into the great hall of the king.

"I have to speak to the King!" Starling shouted at them. But the guards remained firm. It was at this time, that Royal rode up on his horse. He had just returned from a visit to Ella and when he saw the figure of the pirate, the one that he had thought he had killed, he nearly fell from his saddle.

But he dismounted and walked calmly up the stairs where the commotion was going on. His very presence commanded silence. Starling turned to him, but instead of staring at him with the deadly hatred that he had felt previously, he regarded the prince in wonderment. This was his brother. His younger twin? It didn't seem possible.

"What do you want? You know I could take you and have you hung."

"I must speak to King Leander."

"Father does not need to be disturbed by such as you." Royal was not polite, and showed his dislike of the pirate quite openly.

"I have important news for him. Please. Tell him I know of his son." Starling was trying very hard to be pleasant to the cocky prince.

"His son? I am his son."

"I am talking about your brother. Your twin. Just tell him."

Royal was unbelieving. "What are you talking about? What lies have been formulated? I have no brother! I would have been told! Guards take this pirate away – we'll make an example of him for all other pirates. The gallows is the only place for the likes of you."

The guards at the door moved forward to take him, but Starling was quicker and drew his sword. The guards fumbled with their weapons, and in that moment, Starling flung the doors open and rushed inside.

Shouting and curses came from the guards and they stumbled inside after him. Royal followed as well, but Starling's long legs carried him swifter than them all through the hall. He burst past the guards to the throne room and stunned the entire court into silence. He stopped and stared in surprised silence at everything.

"What is the meaning of this?!" The king demanded.

Hot on Starling's heels, Royal rushed in with the guards. They quickly grabbed Starling and pinned his arms behind him, forcing his sword to be dropped.

"Royal! What is this?!" The king demanded again.

"I'm sorry, Father. It's just a renegade pirate that will be properly dealt with."

"WAIT!" Starling hollered, struggling against the men that held him. "I have news of your son! Your first-born son! Prince Royal's twin!"

The king stood and Octavia gasped, clasping her hands over her heart.

"STOP!" Leander commanded. "Release him and let him speak."

The guards cautiously stepped back and Starling walked forward.

"Father? What is the meaning of these preposterous lies? What son? I am your only son!" Royal strode forward towards his parents.

"N-no, Royal, you had a twin. An older brother. He disappeared the night that you were born. We didn't tell anyone about it." Octavia said in a quiet voice as she regarded the young man before her, "What do you have to tell us?" she asked addressing the pirate.

"I am your son." Starling said bowing his head.

A startled gasp rippled through the court.

"Can you prove this?" Leander asked.

Starling pulled a knapsack from off his back. He opened it, and ignoring the velvet pouch that rested on top, he pulled out the signet ring on its chain, the journal entry, and the baby clothes. At sight of all this, a gasp came from Octavia. The king walked slowly down to Starling and took the items. Octavia followed and looked them over as well. When she touched the baby outfit a tear slid down her cheek as she murmured, "Sterling was wearing this when he was taken."

The king and queen studied the tall, silent pirate. "Sterling?"

"It is you." Octavia breathed. "He looked like you, Leander. He still does. This man is our son!"

To all gathered there could be no mistake. With the king and Starling – Sterling – beside each other, everyone could see the resemblance. The young pirate was just a much more youthful version of their king, a bit taller perhaps, but still there was the delicate features, the proud bearing, the black hair, and unmistakably the kind, brown eyes. The king and queen embraced their long lost son joyfully. Royal hesitantly walked forward. He looked confused and unsure. He regarded his brother standing before him. Sterling turned to Royal and they stared in each other's eyes.

"I'm sorry I tried to kill you." Sterling said.

"I'm sorry I nearly killed you." Royal replied. They clasped hands and said at the same time, "Brother." Then they smiled for the first time at each other.

Chapter 20

Word soon spread throughout the entire kingdom of the long lost son of the king and queen returning. Rumors had abounded at the birth of the prince that there had been twin boys and that one had been lost, died, or something else equally horrid. Now that news was out that he was here, everyone was excited to meet him. The king and queen had prepared a huge celebration in honor of him and everyone was invited to attend. After all, he, being the eldest, would be heir to the kingdom. All word that he had been a pirate was not allowed to circulate, and all that was said as to where he had come from was from another land very distant.

Sterling told his family everything – about Captain Albatross and his life as a pirate. He was cleaned up and his hair cut short. His mother insisted that the earrings be removed along with the shabby clothes and other pirate trinkets. No one would have recognized the once former pirate Starling in the new dress and looks of Prince Sterling. Even his tell-tale scar was covered expertly in make-up till it could not be seen.

Of course Cinderella had heard the news, she still hadn't seen him, and with his return Royal hadn't yet visited her. She understood that he would be wanting to spend time with a brother he never knew about and waited for him to come to her. She was sure that she would find out all she wanted to know about Prince Sterling.

"Royal?" the two princes were in the garden talking. The two were always together now. They had become quite close in the week that Sterling had been there, and they were quickly becoming wonderful friends. The fact that they both loved the sea and sailing was the best common ground there was.

"Yes, Sterling?"

"I was wondering… about Cella."

"Cinderella?" the two had not yet mentioned her, and Sterling had thought that they must not have gotten married — yet — since she hadn't been seen around the castle and no one mentioned a princess.

"Yes, are you two married, or are you going to be?"

"Not yet… When we got back she wanted to wait. She— I'm sure that if I asked her she would say yes now. But she didn't want to then. You loved her didn't you?"

"I still do."

"I know she loved you." Royal said quietly.

"Roy, I don't want to intrude. If she loves you now I'll leave. I won't let her see me. I want her to be happy."

"She wouldn't recognize you now!"

"Maybe not. But still…"

"No, she needs to know. I've been thinking a lot about it, Sterling. She loved you, I'm sure she still loves you. She just thinks that you're dead, I want to let her choose. We'll let her know. Or see if she recognizes you. She'll be here tonight."

"I had wondered."

"I'll pick her up in the carriage. She'll be wanting to meet you."

"Yes…"

"Sterling, if she picks you over me know I hold no grudge. I too want Ella to be happy and if happiness is with you, then so be it. Besides, maybe, I'm not ready to be married. I saw Ella and thought I was, but I'm not entirely sure anymore. With you here now, and heir to the throne, Father and Mother won't mind me roving as much as I like. And they'll be wanting you in the books I heard."

"Then they probably don't want me married."

"Nonsense! Ella won't interfere with you learning the ways of the kingdom! And besides, if you're married she'll more than likely be a better way to keep you on shore."

"Perhaps. But Cella is quite a sailor now!"

"Then you can all join me on the seas!"

The two prattled on. They truly had become friends. And soon the night drew closer and the two went indoors to get ready for the celebration. Royal was done quickly and left to get Ella to take to the party. He had given her all the money she needed to buy a dress and this time the Hodgesheds didn't deny her the right to purchase anything she wished. They were going of course, another prince and eligible – also the heir to the throne! Well, Mrs. Hodgeshed wasn't going to miss that opportunity!

"You're beautiful, Ella." Royal helped her in the carriage and sat beside her.

"Thank you." She murmured as she settled beside him, "I've missed our rides. I'm sure you've been busy with your brother though."

"Indeed. I can't wait for you to meet him."

"And I can't wait to meet him. Is he anything like you?"

"Only slightly… Not too much though."

 CB

They soon reached the palace and Royal escorted Ella inside. Prince Sterling was surrounded by people, and even for the other prince, they wouldn't move aside.

The music started, so Royal invited Cinderella to dance and just wait to meet Sterling later. Ella agreed and they went to the floor.

Ella had only caught a glimpse of Sterling, he was taller than anyone else there so he was easy to spot out. His short, black hair complimented his fine, delicate seeming features. "He looks like the king." she thought to herself. He had all the bearing of royalty but his dark brown eyes seemed so familiar.

Ella wasn't paying attention to the dance, she trod on Royal's feet several times, and he noticed her preoccupation. He pulled her aside and questioned, "Are you quite all right, Ella?'

"Oh, yes. I'm sorry, Roy. I was just thinking."

"That's all right."

The song had ended and another began. "May I have this dance?" Royal bowed.

Ella smiled and took his hand letting him lead her onto the floor to try again.

But the song that they were playing caused Ella to falter and lose count, completely forgetting all the steps. Royal paused and saw tears starting to form in her eyes.

"Ella?" he asked in concern.

"I'm sorry, Royal. It's just that— I guess I'm not up to dancing right now. The last time I danced to this song…" she broke off unable to finish.

"We didn't dance to this one." Royal said entirely innocent to the reasons.

"I know. It was on the ship… with Starling."

"I see… Well if you prefer not to dance, we can sit this out."

"Of course she prefers not to dance with *you*." a new voice sounded behind them. Ella's heart skipped a beat – she knew that voice! But how? She turned around and saw Prince Sterling. He looked just like King Leander. However, his eyes, and his voice… Cinderella tried to clear her head, her mind was playing tricks on her. Starling was dead and this prince was not him – no matter what her over strung nerves were doing to her.

"You must be Prince Sterling." she said with a smile.

"I am. And you are Cinderella."

"Yes."

"May *I* dance with you?"

Cinderella wanted to say no, but she was too kind to deny the prince. "All right." she said and took his hand. They started the dance, Royal stood to the side and watched them with a rather sad smile on his face.

"First she steals Prince Royal and now she steals the new prince!" an annoying voice screeched close by where Royal was standing. He turned and saw the plump figure of one of the obnoxious twins. Katherine or Angelica he couldn't figure out who.

"Silence, my dear." Mrs. Hodgeshed said primly, "After all, Cinderella can only have one and her engagement with Royal is an assured thing."

"Not yet. They haven't announced it since she broke it off." the other twin whined.

"Angelica. Katherine. I have said silence. After all, our dear prince is quite close and we wouldn't want him to hear us."

Royal did his best to keep from laughing. He managed stifling it to a snort which he covered with a cough.

Cinderella was amazed at how Sterling seemed to dance just as Starling had. He guided her in exactly the same manner. And the way he stared into her eyes – the look she saw in his brown eyes was just the same. Cinderella stopped and Sterling paused uncertain as to try to start dancing or see what she would do.

"Starling?" she whispered while staring hard at him.

A glimmer flashed in his eyes for just a moment and he said, while leading her back into the dance, "It's Sterling."

Confusion was killing the hope and dreams that had sprung in her mind and she automatically finished the dance. He bowed and smiled. And for just that one instant Cinderella saw a pleading in his eyes. It passed so suddenly that she wasn't sure she had actually seen it. Then he walked away and was instantly swamped with all the ladies trying to get his attention.

"Ella?"

It was Royal. Cinderella turned to him and he led her to the refreshment table where he got her punch.

"Come with me." he took her arm and led her to the patio – away from the noise and people.

"Ella, I have to know. Do you love me?"

"Oh, Roy, I don't know! I thought I did; then I knew I didn't. I might again…"

"Ella. Do you still love Starling?"

"Yes, Roy. I'll always love him…" she looked at the ground not wanting to see the hurt that she was sure was in his eyes.

"What if he were alive?"

"Don't tease me. It is cruel!" she cried out.

"Then you would marry him?"

"Royal, please! I-I don't— I can't talk about him! Your brother, Sterling, is so like him and yet different! His presence has entirely confused me tonight and I can't – don't want to talk of it now. Please understand."

"Then if I asked you if you would marry me—"

"Don't! Not now Royal. Maybe in a week, month, or year. I don't know! But don't be so cruel as to ask me now!"

"I know that you will never love me." he said in a quiet, sad voice.

Cinderella couldn't answer him. Sterling's similarity to Starling had brought him back to mind so much, that she had already started to think the same thing. There was no way she could fool herself into loving someone.

Royal was silent and watched Cinderella. He knew he was right. He felt very sad, for he did love Cinderella; as much as was possible for him to love another person.

"I'll never ask it of you then." he said very softly. He turned away and walked back inside.

Cinderella stood looking out into the gardens. The moon was shedding its silver light over the silent night. She didn't know how long she had been there when the sound of footsteps awakened her listless senses. She half turned thinking it to be Royal, but instead she saw Prince Sterling.

He said nothing and walked to her side. His hands curled over the railing of the patio, just like Starling had always done on the ship. The way he stood there and stared into the garden was also the same as the pirate when he would watch the sunset. He glanced down into Ella's eyes and she knew right then – without any doubts – that here was her beloved Starling.

"Starling." she whispered the name as she stared into the depths of his eyes.

Being outdoors with the absence of the noise and people made Sterling as much like Starling as was possible in his new role in life. He stared into her eyes and bent down quite close to her face.

"Cella." he whispered back as his lips met hers in one much longed for kiss.

෮

"Why didn't you come and tell me you were alive?! I thought you were dead! You truly are the prince? How did— why didn't you tell me?" she cried as she clung to his velvet doublet, refusing to let go lest he disappear from her life again.

His arms encircled her waist and he couldn't take his eyes off of her beautiful face.

"If you let me get a word in I might be able to answer your questions." he said with a large smile.

She blushed but said nothing.

"I was nearly dead. The ship's doctor saved me. Captain Albatross is dead… The doctor told me the truth about my parents. He showed me everything to prove it. So I came back here to claim my place." He paused a moment then said very quietly, "I was afraid that you and Royal had already gotten married."

"I couldn't, Star. Not so soon…"

He hushed her and just held her closer to him in silence.

The guests at the party all started wondering where Prince Sterling had disappeared to. Royal was hard pressed to give Sterling and Ella as much time as he could. He had sent Sterling out to Ella when he had gone inside. He knew it was time that she be told the truth that she had been guessing at ever since seeing him. But he couldn't come up with any good excuses, and his mother and father were wondering where he had gone off to as well.

"Royal, go find your brother, please." Leander said after being told that Sterling was bound to be back soon – maybe.

"Please do, Royal. And where has Ella gone to?" his mother added suddenly noticing the disappearance of her.

Royal blanched and hastily stuttered, "She wanted to be outside, I think it was too stuffy in here for her. I'll go find Sterling!"

Royal left the room as quickly as was allowed a prince and went outside through a side door.

"If you two are quite done everyone is noticing your disappearance."

Cella and Sterling pulled away from each other and he looked rather reproachfully at Royal.

"All this time apart and we are to be denied even this short time?" Sterling asked.

"There will be plenty of time later. For now we have to go back inside to those annoying guests."

They both sighed but Sterling went in and Royal led Ella around to another entrance to the palace and escorted her back to the party.

"We don't want everyone knowing about the three of us right now. It would be sure to cause an uproar."

The rest of the party went wonderfully. Cella and Sterling danced as much as possible – without attracting too much attention. Finally the guests left and the palace returned to the peace of evening.

Chapter 24

"Father. Mother." Sterling walked into the throne room where they were sitting with the court. It was the morning after the party.

"Yes, Sterling." Leander answered.

"I must talk to you. Royal and I actually. Privately."

Leander looked at the court, then shrugging his shoulders, stood, and with Octavia, walked from the room. They went to a private chamber and sat down on the couch to listen to whatever their sons had thought important enough to bring them away from matters of the kingdom.

"We needed to talk to you about an important matter."

"As we assumed. Go on, son."

"Well the fact is Royal is not going to marry Cinderella."

"What?!" Octavia exclaimed.

"Why isn't Royal telling us this?" their father asked.

Royal stood slightly behind Sterling and remained silent.

"It is because I am going to – if she'll have me. Which I know she will."

"I do not believe this!" Octavia said rising. "First she tries to get Royal! Now since he is no longer heir she wants you!"

"Mother!"

"It's true! Why else would she!"

"Because she loved me when she thought me a pirate."

"Explain, son." Leander said, quieting Octavia and pulling her back on the couch.

"It was my ship that she was a prisoner of. She never thought she would get to come home. There with my crew and I she realized that she did not truly love Royal, and we fell in love. When Royal brought her back, she thought I was dead. That is the only reason that she has been with Royal all this time." Sterling paused to fully see the effect that his words were having. His parents were listening attentively. The queen did not seem pleased, but the king seemed accepting of the matter.

"Father, Mother, do you understand? It is not a matter of her wanting anything higher in life – she would still love me if I were only a pirate! It has nothing to do with my inheritance!"

"Yes, Sterling. I believe you. And to be honest, I thought back at the time that she was going to marry Royal that it was only an infatuation and nothing more. I thought I could have been wrong so that is why I said nothing. But heir or not, if you love her and she you, that is all that matters. You have my blessing."

Sterling smiled a large smile and Royal was just as happy for his brother.

Their happiness was short lived for there was a sharp rap at the door. Royal, being closest, walked over to see who it was. Forrest stood there with a paper in his hand.

"Please, Sir, an important message just arrived!"

Royal took the letter and gave it to his father. Leander opened it and quickly scanned the contents. No smile lit his face, and his eyes lost all merriment to be replaced with a hard, coldness.

"Father?" Both brothers asked at once.

In reply he handed the letter to Royal. He looked over it and then read aloud:

"To King Leander of Bleu Evine. Greetings. I hope this note finds you in the best of health. It has come to my attention that you have another son. Congratulations on the safe return of your lost heir. Since the fact that there is now three of you standing in my rightful place as heir to the throne, I must take it upon my shoulders to make sure that I claim the throne before there happens to be more than three. (Meaning before one of your sons marries and has another heir between me and what is mine.) I send this note to give you fair warning – for it is most unpleasant to be taken unawares as to battle. I am sending the majority of my forces by sea – I know your sons love the sea – we will be upon Bleu Evine precisely a week upon your receipt of this letter as long as the weather holds good. Till we meet upon the field of battle. Forever your loving cousin, Augustus."

"Father what is the meaning of this? Who is Cousin Augustus?" Royal asked breaking the stunned silence that had settled over the room.

"Augustus is my cousin that has always wanted the throne. We believed that he was behind the abduction of Sterling, since he was the true heir, but we couldn't find proof to blame him for it. He has apparently decided that he has waited long enough for you, Royal, to die on the seas and for me to die as well. Since Sterling has been returned to us, well there are more of us than he is willing to wait to have die off so it appears he is waging war on us instead."

"Let us meet his forces on the seas, Father!" Sterling said with eyes bright. Here was something he was accustomed to.

"Yes, that might be better than waiting for the battle to come here. Both of you boys shall go by sea, I will take the other troops and take them by land – it will be slower – but we can have you two gone by sunset."

"Sunset?!" Octavia exclaimed. She had been silent this entire time but now the thought of her two boys and husband going to war was too much for her. "No! It's probably a joke. Someone is trying to scare you. You are not all going to leave!"

"Octavia." just that one word spoken in a certain tone of voice from Leander was enough to silence her. She sat watching them all but saying nothing.

"Boys, I will send the captain to gather the troops for you both and a messenger to get your ships prepared.

"Father." Sterling interrupted.

"Yes."

"I have my own ship. It is surely faster than most of yours."

"A pirate ship?"

"Yes, Sir. My crew is loyal to me. They will follow me into this battle."

"I am not sure if that would be a good idea."

"Trust me. I know what I am doing."

"Very well then."

Sterling bowed and Leander sent word to the proper people. In a matter of an hour everything was in motion to get the two princes gone and the rest of the troops prepared to leave in another day or two.

"Sterling." The king pulled him aside before he left for the docks.

"Yes, Father."

"You have enough time to go see her."

Sterling paused a moment, his gaze flickered off to the city. "Thank you." he bowed and ran to the stable. His horse was saddled and he rode quickly to the bakery where he would find Cella.

"Sterling!" she smiled up at him as he entered. He pulled her into his arms hugging her close.

"I came to tell you goodbye."

She pulled back in shock and stared into his eyes, "Goodbye?"

"I have to leave, the kingdom is being attacked. Once all is safe I'll be back and nothing will keep me away then." he pulled her closer again.

"I have to go now." he said breaking the sad silence between them. Neither wanted to part company, but she pulled back and nodded.

"Goodbye, Star."

He smiled wanly and walked back to his impatient stallion. Sterling and Royal rode down to the docks where their ships were ready. Sterling's was still out in deep water so he was conveyed there by rowboat. His crew had done their duty and resupplied the while he had been on shore. He got to the ship, informed the rest of his pirate crew that they were to do battle for the sake of the kingdom and him, and then signaled for the rest of the soldiers to be rowed out. He was right when he knew that his crew would fight for him. They were loyal to their new captain. Everyone had always loved Starling, and that was who he still was. He had even changed from his fine clothes back to the pirate garb complete with kohl, earrings, rings, and medallion.

At the turn of the tide, Royal had his vessel brought up alongside Sterling's and the two brothers set out to rid the seas of the threat to their home.

＃ Chapter 22

A month had passed since the princes' departure. Leander had left three days after them. No news had come from the seas, but Leander was faring well.

Cinderella was walking home from the countryside where she had been walking and dreaming. She went often now since she no longer worked as the scullery maid and had more time to herself. As she was idling along, plucking a few wild flowers from the path and watching the birds fly through the clear, cool air, the distant sound of fire bells reached her ears. Clouds of smoke rolled upwards marring the perfect sky. Cinderella hurried the rest of the way to town to see what was burning. Panic seized her as she got nearer and nearer to the blaze, but it was also closer and closer to her home. She pushed her way through the crowd of onlookers and gave a gasp of fear. The bakery was burning!

"Mother! Father!" she yelled. She grabbed the arm of the person beside her, "Have you seen my parents!" she gasped.

The man roughly shook her off and moved away with a proud look. Cinderella frantically scanned the surrounding crowd, then she saw Mrs. Hodgeshed and her two daughters. She made her way over to them.

"Cinderella! Isn't this a horrible occurrence!"

"My parents!" she panted.

"Oh, I'm sorry, my dear." the woman sneered, "They were caught inside – I haven't seem them get out."

"NO!"

"I'm afraid it's true."

Cinderella stared mutely at the flames licking up the home she knew and loved, but mostly the lives that it had taken from her. The firemen finally quenched the blaze, half the bakery was gone, the other was charred and worth nothing.

A man walked up to Cinderella, she had been pointed out as the daughter of the unfortunates.

"Miss. I'm terribly sorry. We did all we could, but… well… we couldn't get them out… I'm terribly sorry."

Cinderella couldn't say anything. Tears flooded her eyes as she stared at the wreckage of everything she had known and loved. The man let her be and walked away. The onlookers dispersed and Mrs. Hodgeshed put a kindly arm about Cinderella's shoulders.

"Come, dear. You can stay with us tonight."

Cinderella allowed the woman her take her inside and she fell into a fitful sleep.

In the morning there was a memorial service for her parents, no remains of them had been found, but two simple tombstones were set up in the cemetery for them to be remembered by.

When Cinderella got back to town, Katherine met her and took her to the dress shop.

"My dear, I hate to break this to you so soon after your parents' untimely demise, but I must inform you as to certain matters." Mrs. Hodgeshed greeted her.

Cinderella was seated in a chair by the fire where a pig was slowly roasting.

"You see." the woman continued. "Your parents owed me a considerable amount of money. When you were banished they soon fell into harder financial problems and I lent them some of my savings. Since they are gone it falls upon you to pay it off."

"What?"

"I have the letters and everything written out, thoroughly legal, to prove it to you – if you would like."

"Not now… You know though I have no money to pay you!'

"Of course. Now we can have the land to the bakery sold, the profits will come to me to help pay off the debts. Also your parents did name me your guardian in case of their death, so I am your new mother. I feel that since you are now my child and since you owe something to me – well I cannot force you to pay…"

"Please, I do not understand you." Cinderella said. Her mind was so full of grief that she couldn't comprehend what Mrs. Hodgeshed was prattling about.

"Let me say it very plainly. Your parents borrowed a lot of money from me that they never repaid. It is your responsibility to repay it to me now since they are dead. However, I was also made your guardian and so I shall not make you pay it all back to me since you will be my daughter. Though I will take the money from the sale of the bakery land to recompense me in some small way."

Cinderella had nothing to say. She was not a member of the Hodgeshed family and would never consider herself a daughter to that horrible woman. She never thought that her life could get any worse. Sterling was gone – perhaps dead since they still had not heard anything – her parents were dead, her home was gone, and now she was forced to live with the most spoiled twins in the world. But things were only beginning.

Chapter 26

"Cinderella! Hurry up! I'm starving!"

"Cinderella! Wash those dresses immediately!"

"Cinderella! Finish mopping those floors!"

"Cinderella! Come and help me arrange my hair!"

"Cinderella! Finish the sweeping and dusting!"

"Cinderella! Cinderella! Cinderella! CINDER-ELLA!"

All day, every day – there was always something that her two new "sisters" and "mother" wanted her to do. She worked herself nearly to death. She wasn't allowed her own room, so she had to sleep on the hearth which covered her head to foot in soot. Her dress was worn to tatters and completely threadbare. Her eyes were dull, her hair lusterless, her skin pale, and she was very thin since she was given hardly enough to eat. She would get up before dawn to prepare breakfast for the three women. Then she would sweep out the shop before it was opened. After that she would clean, help Angelica and Katherine, cook, clean, help Mrs. Hodgeshed, cook, clean and finally go to bed long after everyone else had retired.

It had been going on for over a month. She was worn out and desperately wanted to get out of this house. But Mrs. Hodgeshed had made it very clear to her – either she accept her place as daughter or repay every penny to her. There was no way she could pay her back. Maybe if Sterling was there and married her he would surely help her, but she wasn't even engaged to him, so she could expect no help from the royalty. Legally, everything that Mrs. Hodgeshed was doing was allowed. Her treatment of Cinderella was not humane, but no one knew because Cinderella wasn't allowed to go anywhere away from the shop.

More time passed, and news came that the war was over! King Leander had succeeded in removing the threat to his kingdom. He returned triumphant. Not too long after the king arrived back, the princes returned, thoroughly pleased with their part in saving their home. Cinderella hadn't heard the news though, she still thought that they were gone – for all she knew Augustus could have taken over the kingdom.

When Sterling landed in Bleu Evine, his first thought was to go find Cinderella, but Royal made him go to the palace or the queen would have a fit. Then there was feasting and celebrating and Sterling was not able to escape to the bakery. The next day, he was informed of the awful news that the bakery had burned down, and no one had seen Cella since that dreadful day.

Sterling rode his black stallion down to where the bakery used to stand, but the reports were correct. The bakery was gone, the land sold, and work was underway to rebuild a new store. Sterling turned with a heavy heart back to the palace. His parents noticed his despondent state, and he told them all what he feared. Rumors were that she had perished with her parents, though others claimed they had seen her watching the fire. He could get no information to match and was totally lost as to what had truly happened to her.

Word was sent out that there was to be a masked ball to celebrate the return of the king and his sons. The queen insisted, saying the kingdom needed to celebrate and masked balls were all the rage in society.

Special invitations were sent out to every house. And it was Cinderella who received the letter at the dress shop. She went to tell her "family" the wonderful news.

"Oh, might I go as well?!" she begged Mrs. Hodgeshed knowing that she would need something nice to wear.

Now the last thing that Mrs. Hodgeshed wanted was for one of the princes to see Cinderella and take her from them. If she had to choose between receiving the money she was due or having Cinderella as her slave, she much preferred the latter.

"I absolutely forbid you to go! There is far too much work for you to do, and there won't be enough time for you to get ready. Most importantly you can't go in those soot covered rags and I have nothing that will be suitable for you."

Cinderella wanted to protest, but there was nothing she could do. She tried to appeal to Katherine and Angelica, but they were worse than their mother. She desperately wanted to see Sterling. The invitation had said "princes" so that meant both of them had to have returned safely. The ball was that evening and without Mrs. Hodgeshed's help there was no way she would be able to have a dress fit to be worn there.

But if Mrs. Hodgeshed wasn't going to let her go to the ball then she would go to the palace now. Cinderella quietly crept from the room where the twins were arguing with their mother over the dresses they were to wear. She had just reached the door and was softly turning the handle to slip outside when Angelica screeched in her awful voice, "MOTHER! Cinderella is trying to leave!"

Cinderella's breath caught in her throat as she froze in place. She couldn't move or turn around. She could hear the woman's tread crossing over towards her.

"So, Cinderella, you think you can just leave without my permission? Where do you think you were going to go?"

She couldn't get her voice to come out. She just stared at the woman's glaring face.

"If you think you can go against my will, you are sorely mistaken." Mrs. Hodgeshed gripped Cinderella firmly by the arm, her claw-like nails digging into her flesh. "I think I will have to make sure you don't try anything like this again." she walked off, dragging Cinderella behind her. They walked up the twisting stairs that led to the attic. Cinderella had only been up there a few times, it was very small and dirty and was only used for storage. Mrs. Hodgeshed opened the door and shoved Cinderella inside.

"Enjoy your stay." she grinned wickedly as she pulled her key ring out of her pocket and found the one for the attic door. She pulled the door closed and Cinderella heard the lock fall into place.

"No!" she shouted as she pounded on the door. How was she going to see Sterling and let him know about her plight? Even if neither of the princes wanted to marry her they would still want to help her. She leaned against the door as tears ran down her face.

The air was stifling, and only one tiny window, that overlooked the back garden, let in any light. She fumbled over the various boxes and crates. Almost everything up here were things that the twins had outgrown – toys and gowns. She made her way over to the window and slid her fingers into the cracks, trying to pry it open to get some fresh air. It was completely sealed shut. She slid to floor and drew her knees up under her chin.

She thought over her life, all the things that happened in so short a time. How she missed everything! Her heart ached to think of never seeing Sterling. She was sure he thought her dead since he hadn't already found her. He had probably been told of the fire as soon as he got back. No one knew she was now under Mrs. Hodgeshed's guardianship. There was no way he could know of her plight unless she was somehow able to tell him!

But could she tell him? Or would it avail anything? The laws in the kingdom clearly stated that any woman, until she is married, engaged, or has her own source of income must be under the care of her parents or legal guardian. And a marriage could only take place if they agreed to the match. Mrs. Hodgeshed would never say yes. If only she had been engaged to the prince before her parents had died. If she had, she would have been given a queenly room at the palace and would be living like royalty until the wedding.

Couldn't the prince bypass the laws though? Wouldn't he be able to command Mrs. Hodgeshed to allow the marriage whether she agreed or not? Cinderella's head hurt from the thinking. But it wouldn't matter. Now that the princes were back, she was sure to be kept prisoner till she died. There would be no way to let him know about her.

The sun was setting and she could hear Katherine and Angelica stomping about while they got ready to go to the ball. She was watching from the window and was able to see when the family left. The carriage house was around back and she saw the twins flouncing about in their velvet, extravagantly embroidered gowns. Masks covered part of their faces and were bedecked in sparkles and feathers. They plopped down into the old family carriage and their mother followed, she paused as she was about to climb into the carriage and glanced up at the solitary attic window. She could see Cinderella's face outlined in the gloom and she gave her an evil grin as she turned and settled herself on the seat across from her daughters.

Cinderella burst into tears, her whole body shaking as she sobbed. Her life was pointless. She would never escape this place. Anger overtook her pain and she stood up, pacing around the small area, kicking the twins garbage out of her way. How dare that woman think she could treat her like this! She picked up a silver hand mirror and hurled it across the room. The crashing of glass met her ears and she gasped as she realized she had broken the window.

She hurried over and knelt carefully on the floor. The majority of the glass had fallen on the rooftop. She found some paper and brushed the fragments together and then leaned her head against the pane, breathing in the fresh air. Tears stung the back of her eyes and she began to cry again.

"My dear, you shouldn't be crying! That only makes your eyes and nose red. It is so unbecoming!"

Cinderella wiped her eyes and looked down into the shadowy garden. A figure detached itself and stepped into the light of the rising moon.

"I don't know if you remember me... When I heard that there was a ball – well naturally I thought of the dear child that I lent the dresses to."

"You! You're the old lady in the cottage!" Cinderella cried happily.

"Yes, my dear. I heard of the fire. But I had seen you in the fields that day so I knew you lived. Then I decided to come look in the city for the girl that couldn't go to the ball because of her dress. See, I found you all right! Now, no time to waste! Let's get you dressed!"

"Oh, but I can't… Mrs. Hodgeshed forbade me to go. She has the right since she's my guardian… Most importantly she locked me in this attic"

"Pish-posh. Tish-tosh! Child when I am through with you no one will ever recognize you – not even that prince of yours! And getting you out of an attic is child's play."

Cinderella was confused, but the old lady walked across the garden and tried the kitchen door, it was unlocked and she let herself in. Soon Cinderella could hear the old lady's footsteps below her and then her slow progression up the stairs. She could tell she had reached the door, but instead of the jangle of keys she heard a strange scratching sound. Then the tumblers of the lock fell away and a tiny head poked out of the keyhole, and then the thing fell out into her lap.

"Why, it's a mouse!" she exclaimed as the old woman shoved the door open.

"Yes, child. It's one of the ones that you saved. I thought I would bring one with me so you could see how well they are doing."

Cinderella smiled at the old woman and the little creature. She gently set it on the floor and it scurried after them as Cinderella and the woman went downstairs. The old lady took them to the twin's powder room and Cinderella waited while the she drew out a bundle from her cloak. She helped Cinderella into the softest, silkiest dress imaginable. It was snow white and swished gracefully about her. Lace trimmed the edges and opals were sewn in the hem. The woman arranged and oiled her hair, making it shine. A golden tiara was placed on her head and a diamond necklace adorned her throat. When the lady was done, Cinderella was totally transformed into a princess. The lady had brought a delicate white mask that she fastened over Cinderella's eyes with a silk ribbon. It was covered in sparkling diamonds and fluffy feathers. No one would be able to recognize her now. She couldn't even tell it was herself in the mirror.

"Thank you!" Cinderella gasped.

"You're welcome, my dear. Now your carriage is waiting out front. Remember to come back at midnight though!"

"Oh I shall!"

The woman showed Cinderella out the front door to where a silvery and gold carriage waited. Snowy spotted, grey horses waited impatiently. The same coachman and footman helped her in.

"Oh my! I forgot all about new slippers!" the lady cried as she saw Cinderella's patched black ones peeping out from beneath the skirt.

"Oh it's all right. I'm sure no one will be able to see. The skirts are more than long enough." she was able to console the old woman and then the driver took her to the palace. It was all so similar to the time when she had gone and met Royal. She wondered if she should reveal herself to Sterling. But if she did then the Hodgesheds would find out as well. She thought better of it and decided to enjoy one night with him – since that was more than she could ever hope for ever again.

While she had been locked in the attic she had remembered how strongly the king was about upholding the law. She knew that if Sterling did ask to marry her, and Mrs. Hodgeshed would surely so no, then the king would never allow the prince to force the woman to allow it. As legal guardian she had every right to decline.

She would rather have Sterling think she had died in the fire than to know she lived and would never be allowed to be together.

When she arrived, no one could take their eyes off Cinderella. Some thought she resembled the girl from so long ago that had won Royal's heart. Others denied any similarity.

Sterling and Royal saw her at the same time and went to greet her with the formality they were required to show all guests. They were dressed as they normally would for their mother's balls, but this time they both wore black masks which did nothing to disguise their identities or handsome faces.

They noticed their mother's gestures that one of them should dance with the beautiful woman. They both bowed and asked, "May I?"

Cinderella so wanted to dance with Sterling, but she accepted Royal's offer and watched Sterling the whole time. When the dance was over, Royal bowed and handed her to Sterling. Something about her was so familiar to him.

Sterling and Cinderella danced the rest of the night together. Neither wanted the dances to end. As he danced with her, Sterling felt like he was once more with Cella. This girl had the exact same way of moving. But if he looked at her his hope would vanish. This girl was so pale, almost whiter than the dress she wore. The more he studied her the more differences he found. The girl wasn't just skinny she was gaunt. The make up and mask tried to hide her hollowed face and sunken cheeks but his sharp eyes were still able to see through it. Her collar bones were far too prominent and in one dance when he was spinning her about, her sleeve had gotten pushed back long enough for him to see dark, purple bruises on her wrist. Her hair seemed clean and healthy, but then he realized it was only oiled and he could see the dull brown showing through in some places. His Cella had so much lighter hair than this girl, it had been almost gold. Everything confused him, but made him also that much more certain she couldn't be Cella.

"You remind me very much of someone I once knew." he commented as the last dance ended.

"Reely? What 'appened to her?" Cinderella replied, she had decided to add an accent to her voice to try to disguise herself all the more from him.

"It would appear she died." Sterling said quietly.

"I'm soooo soary."

Sterling said nothing for a moment then asked, "Please, you haven't told me your name. I would love to know more about my lovely dancing partner."

Cinderella paused, uncertain what as to what she should say, she couldn't tell him, but at that moment she heard the bells of the clock strike midnight.

"Oh! I soary, I moost go!" she turned and fled from the room. Sterling ran after her.

"Wait!" he called. He was definitely faster than her. Just as she reached the top of the stairs to go down to her waiting carriage, Sterling overtook her. He caught her about the waist and refused to let her go.

"You can't just run off like that!" he cried. This girl was even more unusual than she had first struck him as. But as he held her, it hit him again how similar she was to Cella. He couldn't get the thought out of his mind. But how could she be?

"Pleese! I moost go now!" She struggled against his strong arms and he loosened his grip. Her mask had come loose enough that he could see dark hollows beneath her eyes. He was tempted to pull the disguise away from her face, but he couldn't.

He looked so sad, that for a moment Cinderella almost told him the truth. But she didn't want to break his heart or hers yet again.

"Then go." he whispered as he released her.

She turned and ran down the steps. As she did, she tripped and her one of her shoes fell off. She half turned but ran on instead. She could live without it.

Sterling watched her carriage drive away with all haste and he slowly walked down the steps to where her shoe lay. He picked it up and looked it over.

"Strange." he mumbled. "This is not a princess' shoe. It's a working girls." he snorted as he thought of the girl's sickly appearance, there was no way she could have been a princess. He slipped the shoe into his coat pocket and turned to go back inside.

"You know." a voice said from the top of the stair. "This all reminds me of when I first met Cinderella." It was Royal. He had followed his brother outside and had been watching the entire time.

"Really? Cinderella is dead though…"

"You don't know for sure. No one ever said she died in the fire they just said she was gone. Or that she could possibly be dead."

"Then why wouldn't she have told me if it was her!"

"I don't know. Perhaps there's some reason that she couldn't. Perhaps if there were some way to search every house in the kingdom we could see if she's been in hiding or if something has happened to her. I miss her too…"

At that moment, Sterling remembered something he had forgotten about since returning and hearing the news about his Cella.

"I have the prefect solution!" his eyes glowed bright and he rushed inside straight to his chambers, ignoring his parents' calls and the stunned guests.

Royal followed a little later on with more decorum to his parents and guests. When he entered Sterling's room, he saw his brother with his sea trunk. He had insisted on bringing it back from the ship when they had returned from the war. He pulled a velvet bag out and carefully opened it. Inside were two perfect crystal slippers.

"I gave these to Cella, but she forgot them when you – rescued her."

"What good will those do?"

"I'll make a proclamation that the girl that fits this slipper shall marry me!"

"But there's sure to be plenty of girls that wear the same size as Ella!"

"Not these, they're supposedly magic! They only fit the first person to wear them; which is Cella."

"Magic? Where did you come by those?" Roy snorted in disbelief.

"I found them... on one of my pirating adventures."

"You mean you stole them from some hapless merchant."

"They were a trade. The captain of the vessel told me he got them from an enchantress far away. I spared his ship for these."

"Interesting... Well, if it works you might be able to find her... But what if you can't marry her?"

"Why wouldn't I be able to? Unless she's been married off to someone there should be nothing to prevent it."

"Her parents are confirmed dead. If she is still alive there would have to be a new guardian for her. And according to the laws of the land you must have their permission to marry."

"I'll find a way to get past that. Besides who wouldn't want to let her marry me? Oh, I know, it'll be part of the proclamation!"

"We can try it at least."

So the two set to work writing the royal edict Once they were satisfied that it was completed, it read thus:

Royal Proclamation:

Prince Sterling wishes to find a bride. To have the possibility of being chosen, all eligible, young ladies must try on a slipper. If it fits, she will marry the prince, the heir to the throne of Bleu Evine. All parents and guardians must allow the lady that fits the slipper to marry his highness, Prince Sterling. Special couriers will be going round the town to try on the slipper in the next day. Please receive them and do as they ask. And let all, rich and poor alike, try on the slipper.

By Order of his Majesty,
Prince Sterling

"I wonder if it will work."

"If Ella hears, she may not let anyone try the slipper on her. That is if she wishes to stay away from you."

"Never! She would come to me. The only possible reason she hasn't is there is something preventing her ability to – or she is dead…"

"She is alive!" Royal tried to sound confident as he clapped his brother on the back, "This is sure to work – as long as the slipper truly can only fit her foot."

"I hope so."

"Then let us test it before sending out the edict. I'll send Eric to find all the ladies in the palace and have them try on the slipper. If it fits any of them we shall not send out the proclamation."

"Yes! Do that!"

So Royal got Eric and had him find all of the servant ladies in the palace. They met in the royal audience hall and there they each tried on the slipper. None of them fit – even those with feet that Sterling swore looked the same size as Cella's.

"It works." Sterling beamed. So they had the proclamation sent out. Of course the king and queen were very skeptical of the idea. "What if several of the girls do actually fit the slipper? You cannot marry all of them."

"Father, the slipper will only fit Cella. I am positive of this. And if I do not find her this way – well, I suppose I must accept the fact that I shall never see her again."

His parents consented. They wanted their son to be happy. And if this was what would console him to the loss of Cella, then so be it.

Chapter 24

Cinderella had returned to the dress shop and changed into her rags, letting the coachman take the gorgeous gown and mask away. She quickly cleaned up any broken glass that had fallen into the garden and then found a candle and matches to take to the attic. As she walked through the kitchen, she grabbed a loaf of bread and wedge of cheese, shoving them into her pockets. She didn't care if Mrs. Hodgeshed really did keep a strict inventory of her food like she claimed. She was wasn't going to starve. She then found the spare key to the attic and locked herself inside. She hid the candle away incase she should need it later or ended up being locked there forever like she assumed.

She waited up till the Hodgesheds returned, but when no one came to check on her she decided to sleep. Mrs. Hodgeshed came in the morning to make sure she was still in place and left with a sneer.

No food was brought to her all that day. She was glad for the broken window or she was sure she would have suffocated in the heat of the tiny attic space.

Later in the day, Cinderella heard one of the town criers walking through the streets calling out the royal proclamation. Cinderella wondered if Sterling had thought it was her last night. She wondered why he would bother trying this, there were plenty of girls that wore the same shoe size and even more that had the simple black slippers that she had been wearing that night.

Mrs. Hodgeshed was quite pleased by this idea. Surely one of her darling twins would fit the slipper. They had such dainty feet after all.

The couriers went round the kingdom, with Eric in attendance to make sure all was done correctly. They went from house to house, but no girl could fit the gorgeous crystal slipper.

After days of this, people started to complain, others were begging for them to hurry up, and Sterling was getting anxious.

"I think I will go today. I want to see it for myself." he announced. So he rode with the couriers and watched the blushing ladies try on the shoe. Their feet were far too big, far too small, or nearly perfect but not enough. No one fit the slipper. Finally they reached the part of town where Cella's bakery used to be. The prince and his attendants went to the dress shop. They entered and were graciously received by Mrs. Hodgeshed and her daughters.

"Hurry up with them. I would much rather leave." he whispered to the man who had tried the slipper onto countless feet.

"Will one of you ladies please be seated?" the man asked.

One of the twins pranced to a chair and threw herself ungracefully down. She giggled and batted her eyes at Sterling. He hated the sight of her, but kept silent as the slipper was put on. It was much too big for the girl's "dainty" foot. The other twin had the same results.

"Anyone else in the house, Madam?" the man asked in his monotonous voice. "A serving maid or some such girl?"

"No." Mrs. Hodgeshed said firmly.

"Only *her*…" Katherine muttered.

"Cindy…" Angelica pouted.

"Which is it?" Sterling nearly yelled.

"My Prince, Forgive my daughters. We have a very old widow that works in the garden. Surely not at all what you are wanting to waste your time with." Mrs. Hodgeshed said firmly.

Sterling's shoulders drooped and he turned to go.

Cinderella was still locked in the attic. She had only been given cold porridge that morning. Perhaps Mrs. Hodgeshed was going to try to starve her into mindless obedience. But every night she had crept silently from the attic to get herself some bread or fruits or cheese. Thankfully the spare key hadn't been found missing yet.

She had been sitting by the window and had been able to hear the royal attendants arriving. She wanted to go try the slipper on. The proclamation had made it clear whoever fit would have to be allowed to marry Sterling.

The muffled voices slowly drifted up to her. She could tell they were in the dress shop and the twins must be currently trying the shoe on. She cautiously unlocked the door and slipped down the stairs. She could hear them clearer and knew she had only a matter of moments before they left.

Her heart stopped beating as she heard Sterling's voice snapping at the twins. *He* was here too! She paused in the back of the shop. She couldn't see into the front because of the curtain that hung between the rooms, but she heard the unmistakable sound of the door opening and the footsteps of people leaving.

She was too late! She rushed into the kitchen and hurried out of the back door into the garden. She spotted Sterling over the fence. He was mounting his horse and was about to ride away.

Without any thought, she flung the gate open and ran up to him. "Sterling! Please! Let me try it on!" she cried, stopping beside his flighty steed.

He expertly pulled the horse to a standstill and looked down at the pathetic figure below him. She was covered in ashes and her hair was matted and tangled. Her skin was pale and she looked like she needed several meals.

"Where do you live, Maid?" he asked, ready to leave, but having to give all a chance.

"Here. At the dress shop." she stated.

"That's odd. I just came from there and the owner swore that only her, the twins, and a very old widow lived there."

Cinderella paled even more, she was about to say something when a screech came from the shop.

"CINDY!" Angelica – or was it Katherine – yelled.

Sterling turned towards them and in an instant was back inside the shop with Cinderella in tow.

"You lied to me." he spat angrily at the woman.

Mrs. Hodgeshed was visibly shaken and she stuttered, "She's a very poor maid, Your Highness, I didn't even remember her. She's just employed to help round the house at times." she glared in hatred at the girl, wondering how she could have escaped the attic.

The pirate's quick temper had already flared up. How dare anyone lie to him! Though not meaning to be unkind, he roughly pushed Cinderella down into a chair and had the man try the slipper on. The man pulled one of the crystal slippers from the velvet pouch and walked over to Cinderella.

Cella gasped when she saw the slipper. Of course she remembered what Sterling had told her about them being magical and that they would only fit her since she had worn them first. She now understood why he would make that proclamation. Unexplainable fear gripped her – but then relief. The slipper would fit and she would be free!

The man lifted her foot which was already bare and covered in dirt. He grimaced and then slipped the shoe on. An astonished silence filled the room as everyone saw quite plainly that the slipper fit perfectly.

Sterling came round to the front and kneeled down to see her face. "Cella?" he asked hoarsely.

She looked away and said hurriedly, "Th-there must be a mi-mistake… I don't—" she suddenly didn't want him to know it was her. She didn't want him to see the dreadful state that she was in.

Sterling shushed her with a finger to her lips and turned her face so he could fully see her. "Cella, is it truly you?" he couldn't believe that the girl he had fallen in love with could turn into this.

She blinked back tears that threatened to spill over. He gazed deeply into her eyes, and instantly knew in his heart that indeed this girl, even though she so wasted away, was his Cella.

"Tell me." he commanded in a quiet voice.

"Oh, Star!" she sobbed. "I wanted to! But—"

She was silenced once more by Sterling, but this time with a very gentle kiss.

Everyone stood by or shuffled their feet in an embarrassed silence. Sterling finally drew away and pulled Cella up with him. He turned angrily upon Mrs. Hodgeshed and commanded in steely tones, a voice he rarely used but all of his crew knew never to disregard him, "Explain the meaning of this outrageous behavior!"

So she told the prince about the debts, the guardianship she had over Cinderella, and everything else as delicately as possible. Sterling then made Cinderella tell him her side and she spared none of the true facts. Sterling was livid with rage, and the pirate in him would surely surface again if it hadn't been for Eric standing nearby.

"My Lord, Prince. Let us take them to your father for him to meet judgement upon this woman and her brood of like-minded children."

Sterling agreed and they were put into the carriage. Cella, though, he placed on his stallion and rode behind her. She laid against him and watched the town pass by in a blur. Then the palace appeared and he dismounted, pulling her down into his arms.

ଔ

King Leander agreed that the debts legally did need to be paid. However he said that the way Cinderella was treated as a "daughter" of Mrs. Hodgeshed was entirely unlawful and therefor, all debts that Cinderella owed to the woman had better be cancelled for the work she had done. He claimed that it far exceeded the owed amount. Because of the ill treatment the guardianship was removed. Of course, legally, Cinderella still required a guardian, so she asked if it could be transferred to the kindly woman in the cottage.

The king sent someone to retrieve the old woman. When she entered, the queen was shocked that Cinderella knew her for this was the queen's very own godmother! The old lady was more than happy to be guardian of Cinderella and so the papers were drawn up. The king dismissed the court, satisfied that everything had been handled according to the law.

Right there, after all was announced, Sterling walked up to Cella and in his loud, clear voice, dropped to one knee and said, "Cella, Cinderella, won't you marry me?"

"Yes!" she cried as she flung her arms about his neck.

He twirled her about the room, kissing every inch of her face.

The old woman watched them with a smile on her face and once he had set the girl on her feet she walked over to them. The prince coughed, realizing he should have asked the woman first. But she only laid a wrinkled hand on each of theirs, smiling up into the flushed faces.

"There could be no better match in all the kingdom. You have my blessing, dear children."

Sterling insisted that Cella be examined by the royal physician who assured him that she would be fine with proper nourishment, rest, and a bit of sunlight.

Sure enough, after Cella had been installed in the palace with a room of her own, she began to show signs of her old self.

Sterling wanted her to be completely recovered before their wedding and so they set the date to be two months away. It was more than enough time to have preparations made.

Chapter 25

Wedding bells broke the still, afternoon air. Everyone that could was at the cathedral where the wedding of Prince Sterling and Cinderella was taking place. Never had there been such a reason for a celebration than there was that day. Everyone had a day off from any type of labor, and those that were high enough in society were present at the wedding.

Cinderella had never looked so elegant nor beautiful. The old woman had introduced Cinderella to the duchess, surprisingly the queen's mother, who took such a liking to the girl, that she had her own personal tailor create the most astonishing wedding gown imaginable. It was the creamiest white, with lacy ruffles and layers of silk skirts. It was glittering with the smallest gem stones that turned a myriad of colors when they caught the light. A silver frontlet adorned her brow and held the veil in place. Her hair was arranged to compliment her lovely face to perfection. She wore the queen's gift to her, the emerald necklace. It did not match her attire perfectly, but the queen was touched to see the simple adornment about Cella's throat.

Sterling thought she had never been so beautiful, absolutely elegant and innocent. He was dressed in all that was required of nobility; the finest velvet tunic and doublet, a fur-lined cape that reached to the floor, and the frontlet that was the prince's to wear. No sign of the pirate he had once been showed through.

They were married, and everyone showered them with well-wishes.

Sterling and Cella had decided that they wanted to go to Fleur Shea for their honeymoon. He had declared that only his former pirate crew and ship were worthy enough to take them there.

They were conveyed to his vessel and the crew were elated to see Cella and their captain together at last, and once more sailing with them. Even though they had been pirates, they were now true gentlemen. Sterling had decided to keep this ship as his own for any private sailing along with his crew, who were no longer pirates. He paid them far more than they could ever have hoped to plunder, and they were ecstatic to still be in the service of the new prince.

Fleur Shea was as beautiful and enchanting as Cella remembered it. They stayed in the cabin that used to be Sterling's home, and they would wander the shore at sunrise and ride their horses all over the island.

Sterling could not forget about Captain Albatross, the man he had always thought to be his father. Being on the island only served to remind him even more. Cella found him early one morning whittling some holes through one of his shells. She watched as he finished, threading a leather cord through the holes he created. He tied if off and slipped it over his neck with the other medallions and necklaces that he had taken to wearing upon their return to the island.

"What is that?" she questioned him.

He had felt her presence when she had first come up and knew she had been watching him. He stared out at the turquoise waves while he fingered the shell.

"This was the first shell that Captain Albatross found with me. I want something to remember him by. The king may be my father, but he will never replace the captain. You understand the loss of parents… I grew up with him my entire life. This place just reminds me so much of him…"

Cella walked closer and wrapped her arms around her husband. "You don't have to try to explain."

He hugged her back then led her down to the shore where they could watch the sunrise and then get a meal at the town inn.

༺༻

Once they had safely returned to Bleu Evine, Royal was allowed to leave on a voyage once more with Eric. Sterling was forced into reading almost every book in the royal library until he knew the entire history and everything to do with ruling the kingdom.

Cella was happy to be a princess, and she was always very kind to her ladies in waiting and all of the maids that worked there.

The queen quickly grew to love Cella and couldn't fathom how she could have resented the girl so much as to have her banished.

The entire kingdom was thrilled to have her as their princess and future queen. Sterling was sure to become a great king like his father and no one resented the fact that he had been a pirate. Of course a secret like that was bound to leak out eventually. But if anything it added to his appeal with the commoners. He knew what it was truly like to live by his wits and with lowly means.

And now, we've come to the end of the story.

King Leander ruled Bleu Evine to the end of his days and the throne passed to the prince, King Sterling. He ruled wisely with his darling Cella by his side.

Royal was almost always at sea – voyaging and exploring. He eventually found a girl, a supposed island princess, that had always lived on and by the sea. They fell in love and he married her. They stayed out to sea most of the time, and both were extremely happy.

Once Royal was married, Eric was finally allowed to stay at Bleu Evine. He married the handmaiden that he had always loved, and they were extremely happy together. Eric took over the role of personal valet, bodyguard, and friend to Sterling, and his wife was the nearly the same for Cella.

William was not forgotten for the help he had provided and his friendship with Cella. He was made captain of his own ship and often sailed with Royal when his presence and knowledge of the seas was desired. He never married, since he had lost his heart to Cinders, but he was content and happy being where he loved on the sea and finally being off the dreaded prisoner ship.

Mrs. Hodgeshed and her daughters left Bleu Evine and settled somewhere that their name had not been heard before. The news of the horrible treatment that they had inflicted on Princess Cella was gossiped all about and everyone refused to buy any more gowns made by such an evil woman. Mrs. Hodgeshed opened up shop again in the new town and was able to do just fine with the income and the remaining money Mr. Hodgeshed had left her.

Katherine was married to a duke that lavished her with all the presents her greedy heart could desire. Angelica was married to a lord who treated her very much the same as Katherine's husband. Both girls were pompously happy and drove their poor husbands, who had been so blindly stupid as to marry them, nearly insane and bankrupt.

The duchess was often at the palace and Cella enjoyed entertaining her. She always had the most interesting tales to tell of the other kingdoms she had visited.

The old lady insisted that she be allowed to live in her cottage with the mice that Cella had rescued. Sterling and Cella often visited with her. She was given anything and everything she could ever use and lived happily for the rest of her days.

King Sterling and Queen Cella lived happily in Bleu Evine. Every year they would go to Fleur Shea and stay in the cottage for at least a month. It was only at these times that Cella was able to see her husband as she had first met him; the tall, commanding pirate. He would wear his old clothes and look just like the pirate bosun he had been those many years ago.

They eventually had twins, a boy and a girl, Prince Majesty and Princess Grace. Majesty was the heir to the throne and was just like his father. He loved the sea and had a quick temper like the pirate Sterling had once been. Grace was rightly named for she had all the gracefulness of a lady and was as sweet tempered and kind as her mother.

And they all lived happily ever after.

The End

About the Author

Heartless has been writing stories their entire life. When not writing, they can be found playing with their four cats, gaming, or creating arts and crafts.

Heartless is working on several other books and has just announced that *Rain, A Tale of Snow White* will be the next story in their fairy tale series.

Made in the USA
Columbia, SC
05 May 2018